DUDLEY PUBLIC LIBRARIES

The loan of this book may be renewed if not required by other readers, by contacting the library from which it was borrowed.

D1429182

000003057669

The
Key to
finding
Jack

Ewa Jozefkowicz grew up in Ealing, and
studied English Literature at UCL. Her
debut novel *The Mystery of the Colour Thief*,
published by Zephyr in 2018, was shortlisted
for the Waterstones Children's Book Prize. Her
second book, *Girl 38: Finding a Friend*, blends
contemporary times with WWII Poland.
Ewa lives in north London, with her husband
and twin daughters.

Also by Ewa Jozefkowicz

The Mystery of the Colour Thief
Girl 38: Finding a Friend

The
Key to
finding
Jack

Ewa Jozefkowicz

ZEPHYR
An imprint of Head of Zeus

First published in the UK by Zephyr,
an imprint of Head of Zeus, in 2020

9 7 5 3 1 2 4 6 8

A catalogue record for this book is available
from the British Library.

ISBN (HB): 9781789543568
ISBN (E): 9781789543506

Cover artwork © Katy Riddell

Printed and bound in Great Britain
by CPI Group (UK) Ltd, Croydon CR0 4YY

Head of Zeus Ltd
First Floor East
5–8 Hardwick Street
London EC1R 4RG

WWW.HEADOFZEUS.COM

One

'So listen to this one. You have a treasure chest that you want to send me in the post. Each of us has our own padlock with a key, but you don't have the key to my padlock and I don't have the key to yours. How can you send me the treasure chest and make sure nobody else can open it?'

We were sitting on Jack's bed, staring out through the skylight. I was supposed to be in my own room fast asleep, but I'd sneaked up the stairs as I did so often.

Being six years older than me, Jack stayed up until whatever time he wanted, and he was hardly ever asleep when I crept in.

That night I could already hear the familiar engine roar. I knew without checking the clock that it was the 10.15 p.m. flight to New York. Right on cue, the flashing dot appeared in the black square of Jack's skylight. I liked to imagine all the people sitting in the plane waiting to reach their destination. I even made up stories about them. The old lady going to visit her businessman son, who'd recently started working in Manhattan. A newly married couple off on their honeymoon – drinking champagne and kissing. And, in the row in front of them, a family with loads of kids coming home after spending a few weeks in London over the summer holidays. The stewardesses were a bit annoyed because the kids kept getting out of their seats and running up and down the aisle, colliding with the food and drinks trolleys.

I tried to focus my mind on Jack's riddle.

'Easy. I would send you the key in a separate envelope. Only you and I would know what it's for,' I declared triumphantly.

'Nah. Come on, Flick, you can do better than that. It could easily be intercepted.'

I racked my brain.

'Oh, I don't know. Crack the padlock open with

a hammer?' I asked, although I knew it was the wrong answer.

'You have to be subtler than that. If it's possible to force it open, anyone could. Think harder, sergeant.'

We had a joke from when we were little that Jack was a detective doing lots of undercover work, and I was his main contact in the police force. He'd explained that this role was much more important than being his assistant (which I always wanted to be), because it meant heading up the detective operations in the field. 'The difference is that all your work is legal. Some of what I do is undercover and shady. Together we make a great team though.'

The roles were perfect, because I loved to follow rules and Jack hated them. One of his absolute favourite things was to make people laugh. He often got away with his practical jokes, and when he didn't, he got detentions. Quite a lot of them. That made Dad really cross, especially now, as Jack was supposed to be concentrating on his work and getting into uni. Then Mum would be cross because Dad was cross, and normally Mum was on Jack's side. Dad said she was over-protective of him. But Jack was also cleverer than anyone I knew and could solve the hardest puzzles and mysteries in seconds.

'Remember that working out a riddle might take a few steps. Let me start you off. You have your own padlock with a key. You send me the chest with your locked padlock attached. I receive it, but instead of trying to open the chest, I add my padlock to it, also locked. Then I send it back to you. Is it beginning to make sense? You'd be receiving the same chest but this time with two padlocks.'

'Of course! I unlock my padlock and send the chest back to you with only your padlock attached, and you can unlock it and get the treasure!'

He held up his hand for a high five. Jack was like that – helping me towards the answer but making me feel I'd got there myself.

He passed me his box of chocolate frogs and I sucked on one happily, even though I'd brushed my teeth. At first the mix of minty toothpaste and chocolate was disgusting, but I knew that after about thirty seconds my mouth would be filled with caramelly wonder.

Each time I cracked one of Jack's puzzles I immediately felt sleepy and he had to pinch me to send me back to my own room. But that night I was determined to stay awake for as long as possible, because it would be the last time in ages we'd be able to have this kind of conversation face to face. In the corner of his room, by the window, my brother's rucksack was already packed, and his passport and plane tickets were lying on the bedside table.

Jack would be gone for a whole ten months. He wouldn't be with us when we went to the fireworks for my birthday in November. He wouldn't bring me huge sticks of marshmallows like he did every year and tell me the names of all the weird and wonderful flashes in the sky. I could never tell which were real and which he'd made up on the spot.

He'd also miss Christmas. Grandma Sylvie would come round, as she did every year, and complain about her aches and pains, and without Jack, there would be nobody to distract her by suggesting a card game, or giving us all some really complicated puzzles to solve.

I tried not to think about it too much, because it made a painful ball, which I couldn't swallow, form in my throat.

So as I sat there, looking up at the skylight, I tried to think about everything other than Jack leaving, which was easier said than done. I told myself that I would remember this evening as 'The Night of the Treasure Chest' because otherwise it would have to be 'The Night Before Jack Left'.

I kept replaying the short birthday greetings film that Jack had sent me from Brazil. It was strange seeing him there on the beach, when Mum and I were in the middle of our Christmas shopping. We went to Uncle Michael's for New Year's Eve dinner and when I lit my sparkler, I made a couple of important resolutions. The first was that I would finally complete at least one of the stories that were swarming in my head, inspired by Jack's riddles. The second was that I would persuade Dad to pay for us all to visit Jack.

On the wall calendar that he'd made for me, I kept counting down the days that he'd been away and fortunately, time was passing quite quickly. The new term started and we were set an exciting writing project in English. Otherwise, life carried on as normal. There were no signs that everything was about to change. Even the flashing lights of the 10.15 p.m. to New York still sped reliably past Jack's skylight night after night. But then, halfway through January, the boy who used to lie watching them was somewhere on the other side of the world, caught in what the lipsticked newsreader on TV said was 'one of the worst natural disasters in living history'.

 **Two**

It was a Thursday afternoon in the middle of English class. We'd been reading *Sherlock Holmes and the Case of the Silk Stocking*, and Mrs Emmett had set us the best possible assignment – to write our own detective story. My discussions with Jack had given me so many great ideas. I'd even jotted some down in a special book of 'riddle tales' which I kept under my bed. I promised myself that one day I would type them up on Mum's laptop – I just hadn't found the time to do it yet. Now, after only half an hour, I'd managed to fill more than three pages.

Keira was sitting next to me, twisting one of her braids round and round her finger and biting her tongue in concentration. I glanced at her exercise book and saw that she'd written a short paragraph which had more words crossed out than left in.

'Oi, stop copying,' she whispered, winking at me. Keira and I had been friends since nursery and we were good at completely different things. I love English, history and geography – anything that involves a story, while Keira is great at maths and science, and likes things that have a definite answer. Being friends means we can help each other with stuff the other person isn't so good at.

'I can't think of a story to save my life,' she whispered to me now. 'D'you think anyone will notice if I adapt one of the episodes of *Crime Fighters* that I watched with Mum the other week? It's on a weird channel. Probably not that many people would have seen it.'

'Go for it,' I told her.

'Everyone busy with their work?' said Mrs Emmett, raising her eyebrow at us. 'I see that some of you have lost your concentration. Before we finish for the day, it might be helpful to hear your opening paragraphs. I want to feel that dramatic tension and the slow revealing of clues that Arthur

Conan Doyle is so good at. Does anyone want to volunteer?'

Her question was met with silence.

'All right, *I* will,' said a low voice with an American accent from the back of the class.

'Thank you, Duncan. Come to the front.'

'Do I have to? I can read sitting down.'

'You'll be able to project your voice better facing the class.'

Duncan seemed to take ages getting to the whiteboard. His best friends and sidekicks, Max and Elliot, slapped him on the back for good luck.

As always, everything about him looked immaculate. His shoes were clean, his trousers barely had a crease, and his shirt was tucked in. Even though I couldn't see his exercise book from here, I sensed that he probably had super-neat handwriting.

'His dad's a famous author. He's won some important awards,' Keira had told me when Duncan had joined our year. 'Mum's read all of his books. And Duncan's brother is amazing at tennis. He's only in sixth form and he's already won a couple of junior tournaments.'

Duncan certainly acted as though he had his own part to play in his family's fame. He walked through the school corridors with his head held high, like a celebrity on the red carpet, and he barely spoke to anyone except his two best friends. It was as if the rest of us weren't worth his attention.

Today, he didn't even raise his eyes to look at the class. Instead, he cleared his throat and shifted his weight from one foot to the other. There was a long silence during which he seemed to be thinking.

'This one is called "The Cabin",' he said eventually. 'It's about... a dead man in a cabin. You'll see.'

He read confidently, and did his characters in different voices, but it was obvious that his story hadn't been well thought through. A body was discovered in a cabin in the middle of a snowy forest. A detective was called to the scene and found that there were no windows and the only door was locked from the inside. When he forced his way in, he saw a man with a stab wound in his neck and a bucket of bloody water beside him, but nothing else.

I could tell straight away what had happened. It was a variation of a riddle that Jack had told me years ago. The man had been stabbed with an icicle. I rolled my eyes at how obvious the answer was.

Duncan must have spotted me as he finished reading because I could see a pink glow in his freckled cheeks. His eyes narrowed slightly. I knew that look.

'Thank you, Duncan. A promising start. There's certainly some impressive characterisation. I think you could work on building the suspense. We have time for a couple more. Any other volunteers?'

I avoided Mrs Emmett's gaze, but I should have known that this was the wrong tactic. Jack used to have her for English and he'd warned me that she always picked on the people who least wanted to be chosen.

'Felicity? Do you want to come and share the opening of your story with us?'

I nodded, even though I hated reading my work aloud. I could feel Duncan's gaze on my back as I walked to the front of the class, and I made a point of looking straight at him before I started reading. As always, he refused to catch my eye.

'It's because he likes you,' Keira insisted. 'I mean, really *likes* you. I've seen him looking at you when he thinks you won't notice. Why else would he do that?'

But I didn't agree with her. Duncan was just strange and it was probably his way of trying to make me feel uncomfortable.

I still remembered the moment we'd met on the first day of term last year.

'So your name's Flick?' he'd asked, when we were walking down a corridor between lessons.

'Yes.'

'It's peculiar, isn't it?' he asked and I couldn't tell whether he was making fun of me or if he was really curious about it.

'It's short for Felicity,' I explained, although I'm sure he knew that.

'I'm Duncan. I've recently moved over from Florida,' he said in his American accent, which only added to the impression that he was genuinely famous. 'And where are you from?'

'I'm local,' I told him, 'I grew up here and I went to Ellerton Primary.' I instantly felt like the least interesting person in the world. That was the thing about Duncan – even if he said very little, he managed to get under your skin.

Today I tried to ignore him and cleared my throat awkwardly.

Lady Abigail Jackson hated Christmas shopping. Every year she thought about sending one of her maids instead. What she wouldn't give to avoid the tedious crowds, the gridlock of horses in the streets and the freezing cold. But she always ended up going herself, much to her household's dismay. It was partly because she had no idea what to buy and also because she didn't trust anybody else to do the job well.

The children, of course, insisted on going with her. They wanted to see the huge Christmas tree outside St Paul's Cathedral and to visit the new chocolate shop that had opened on Cheapside. Margot had worn her new red beret for the day and Henry flew out of the house with no coat, so his sister had to chase down the road after him.

There were even more people in the streets than she'd expected. It took them an age to cross Blackfriars Bridge, as the children kept stopping to admire the view of the Thames on this crisp December morning.

'Mother, there's a carol service at St Bride's,' said Margot, pulling her sleeve. 'Can we go and see, just for a minute?'

Lady Abigail agreed. After all, Margot didn't often get a chance to enjoy herself.

Ever since Lady Abigail's husband had died four years earlier, she'd put her efforts into making sure her children were well set up for life, and that Margot in particular knew how to take care of herself. She had struggled after his death, but she'd learned how to manage the servants and the estate, how to do the accounts and take charge of her children's education. In addition to Margot's regular lessons with her private tutor, she received guidance on how to be 'a proper young lady'.

When they reached the church, Lady Abigail grabbed Henry's arm to stop him from making a run for it. Luckily the little rascal seemed overwhelmed by the crowds pouring down the narrow lanes to St Bride's and was sticking close to her. But when she turned back to look at the choir, she realised that she couldn't see her daughter.

'Margot!' she screamed. 'Margot!' The crowd around her shifted, alarmed by the volume of her voice. 'Have you seen my daughter? She was wearing a red beret.' The women around her shook their heads, the men parted to let her pass. The sound of the choristers stopped. She was aware of people joining the search. They shouted questions. 'How old is she? What colour hair? How tall?' She answered them quickly, her eyes scanning the church.

Then, above the heads of the crowd, she saw a red beret being passed to her. When her fingers closed upon it, she felt a sudden pricking sensation. Attached to a pin was a piece of card showing a tiny picture of a bell.

'It was lying by the front steps,' said an elderly lady.

Lady Abigail stayed at the church long after the crowds had left, and spent hours walking the streets of London shouting her daughter's name. But Margot was nowhere to be found.

I'd meant to stop reading much sooner, but somehow I'd managed to reach the end of what I'd written. When I looked up, I saw rows of faces staring at me expectantly.

'That's sensational,' said Mrs Emmett. 'I'm honestly lost for words.' She was looking at me with an expression I'd never seen before.

'I want to know what happens next,' I heard one of the boys in the front row whisper.

'Well, you'll be pleased to know that homework is composing your next chapter,' said Mrs Emmett. 'If you're keen, you're welcome to post your work on the class intranet for others to read. If Felicity decides she wants to do this, you'll all have a chance to read her next instalment.'

'It's a bit weird to have lessons in being a "young lady",' I heard Duncan say. 'Was that actually a thing?'

'In Victorian England that was quite common in wealthy families,' said Mrs Emmett. 'They wanted to ensure their daughters would marry well and the best way to do that was to teach them how to behave appropriately and attractively in society. Of course, things are very different for girls and women now.'

I looked in Duncan's direction, interested to see how he would take this response.

But I didn't get a chance to find out, because at that moment there was a knock on the door and Mrs Lyme, the school receptionist, came in.

'Felicity Chesterford? Could you come to Mrs Singh's office?' She was trying to keep her voice steady, but I could sense that something bad had happened.

Three

I followed her along the corridor to the head's office and, when she opened the door, I saw Dad. There he stood in his work clothes, but they were wet and his hair was plastered to his forehead.

'What are you doing here? How come you're soaked?' I asked.

He looked down at his drenched clothes as if he'd barely noticed them, and then I saw the fear on his face. I'd never seen him scared before. He was always in control – it was part of his job as a barrister to be logical and never emotional. I didn't know what was going on.

'It's Jack,' he said. 'There's been an earthquake in Peru, near Lima. It happened early this morning. We didn't want you to hear about it and worry.

Mum and I haven't been able to get hold of him yet, but I'm sure we will.'

'What?' I laughed in disbelief. Time slowed down.

Suddenly, something in my stomach jolted. It was that feeling you get before you're going to be sick. I pelted through the door and into the nearest toilet, where I retched until there was nothing left in my stomach. Afterwards, I slumped against the door and breathed in greedy mouthfuls of air. The strip lights on the ceiling multiplied before my eyes.

I knew that I couldn't go back to class. I returned to the head's office where Dad was waiting for me. I took his hand in the way that I'd done when I was much smaller, and together we walked to the main doors, both feeling bewildered. I could see through the windows that it was still raining heavily. It was as if the world knew the awfulness of the news we'd been delivered.

'Do you want to get the bus?' I muttered to Dad.

'Let's walk,' he answered quietly.

After signing out at reception, we left, passing the blur of brick that was the new primary school, and the fields where we'd played football with Dad when we were younger. I focused on my feet, black smudges against the squelchy green and brown. Raindrops nestled in my hair and then trickled their way slowly down the back of my neck.

'He's going to be all right though? Isn't he? They'll find him and he'll be all right?' I asked Dad desperately. Of all people, Dad would know what to do. He'd dealt with some very tough cases. Surely, he would be able to make this OK too.

He took a long time to answer – unbearably long.

'I don't know, Flick,' he said eventually in a voice that didn't sound as if it belonged to him at all. 'The truth is that I don't know.'

My chest contracted. We walked on and on through the streets until eventually the rain stopped and we reached our scratched red front door. I noticed I'd been clutching Dad's hand so tightly that his knuckles had turned white.

'Mum's home,' he said. But for some reason, instead of ringing the doorbell, I got out my keys.

I made straight for the stairs. There was only one place I needed to be. I ran up all three flights without bothering to take off my shoes. When I reached the top floor my feet stopped at the threshold of his room.

I'm not sure what I expected to see. Jack's room greeted me in silence. Dust particles danced. I'd always come in without knocking, but today it felt wrong. I had to stop my hand from rapping on the doorframe.

There was something about his room that I'd always loved. It wasn't the size – although, apart from the living room, it was the biggest room in the house. Jack had the whole top floor to himself. Dad said that an artist had lived in the house before us, and he'd converted the attic into a studio, with a skylight and a window overlooking the street and the river beyond, and a little seat on the ledge where he could look out and ponder the world.

The place was messy but cosy, with Jack's stuff still lying around. There was the soft smell of chocolate and washed sheets mingled together, and the spotted rug that always flipped upwards like a curl of hair.

'Howdy,' I said into the quiet. I forced my right foot inside and slowly made my way to the bed. I took out my phone and called Jack. It went straight to voicemail. I tried again a minute later with the same result. I hadn't really expected him to answer, but I felt a sudden, desperate need to hear his voice. I replayed the video clip he'd sent me on my birthday when he was on the beach in Brazil. His nose was so sunburned that it had begun to peel. He was lying in a deckchair, eating watermelon. He seemed relaxed and happy, but there was a tiny shake in his voice when he said he missed us.

I lay face down on the duvet and breathed in deeply. It wasn't as strong as before, but I could still smell that faint sweetness. Then a thumping began in my head, like a tiny drummer beating a fierce, sad rhythm. My hand reached and felt for the roughness of the chocolate frog packet. Out of the corner of my eye, I spotted a hair – a single, blond strand, short and thick.

I stared and stared at it, until my vision blurred. Picking it up carefully between my thumb and forefinger I looked for something that I could put it in. Suddenly, there was nothing more important than making sure that hair was safe.

I scanned Jack's desk. Then I kneeled down and peered under the bed – which was home to his most prized possessions – half-empty packs of cards (used for some of his more imaginative tricks), scrapbooks of ideas and pictures of friends and people he admired.

When he was younger, my brother used to take his scrapbooks with him everywhere, even to school. He sketched his funny tricks, jokes he'd invented and notes on how to bring them to life.

I could vividly remember his first detention. He thought it would be funny to put plastic cups of water along the corridor. When everyone came out of class, they had to navigate their way to their next lesson via a huge obstacle course. Obviously loads of water spilled in the process and the corridor soon became very wet. When somebody else was about to get the blame, Jack owned up. That was something everyone knew about him – he would never lie, and he always took responsibility for what he did.

Mrs Singh was a great head and Jack didn't always get caught. But his tricks didn't stop and after many incidents, she must have written Mum and Dad a strongly worded email because Dad sat Jack down for 'a chat'. Mum was at her after-work yoga class, which was a shame. She never liked any of us arguing. Without her there, I didn't want to leave them alone in the kitchen, so I sat on the counter and waited to see what happened.

'Why did you do it?' Dad demanded. 'You're sitting your exams. You need to be revising. The competition out there is tough,' he said, pointing randomly towards the window. I almost expected to see a queue of keen future barristers in our garden. 'If you want to get onto your law course, you can't be messing around at this stage.'

'I'm sorry,' Jack muttered. He sounded strangely young in front of Dad. He swept his long fringe out of his eyes, something he did when he was nervous.

'It seems as if you have no self-discipline,' said Dad, which I thought was unfair, because Jack was extremely well-organised and on the whole very careful. He had to be, having haemophilia. It was a disease that meant his blood didn't clot in the way that other people's did. He bled for a long time after injuries and bruised easily, and he could be in deep trouble if he ever got internal bleeding. Jack had to have injections every other day to help with his clotting, and for years he'd managed them himself.

I felt like pointing this out to Dad, but it was probably the wrong time.

'If you're feeling stressed or need help you can ask,' he said to Jack now, 'but don't resort to this silliness. You could have spent that useless detention writing your personal statement for your uni application. You'd better get onto that tonight. Don't waste time planning practical jokes, Jack – they're not funny.' It wasn't true, of course. His classmates found them hilarious. I bet he had brightened up everyone's day.

I was shocked when Jack didn't say anything. He was normally the first to argue with Dad when it came to stuff like sport, the environment, or things on the news – they seemed to have such completely opposite opinions about everything. But on this subject, Jack was silent. He nodded, then turned and ran up the stairs.

Watching Dad with Jack made me wonder how he would react if I told him I hoped to become a writer one day. What if he wanted me to be a lawyer too? I made a mental note to tell him soon that law wasn't something I was interested in.

Dad's reaction got worse after each detention, because Jack kept getting them – he couldn't seem to resist plotting new tricks. But then he got his mock exam results the following January, and I knew our parents were secretly amazed at how good they were. I was the only one who wasn't surprised. Jack had always done incredibly well at most things without having to put in much effort.

I snapped out of my daydream when I saw it, peeking out from under the bed, almost asking to be picked up – a small, black, glossy box with a pink flamingo on top. I recognised it immediately. It had been given to Jack on his twelfth birthday by Grandpa. I remembered Jack showing me the card that went with it.

To keep all your treasures in, it had said.

I opened it – the perfect place for that lonely strand of hair. But it turned out that Jack had already used it as a hiding place for one of his treasures: a beautiful, fine gold chain with a small key attached.

It was the key he had always worn around his neck. I didn't know he'd parted with it when he went travelling, but here it was, separated from him, lying on a bed of cotton wool. A scrap of paper was tucked beside it.

For S.F. to keep until I'm back, it read.

I'm not sure how long I sat there staring at the tiny key, rubbing it between my thumb and index finger. It could have been minutes or hours. Time seemed to hang suspended now that Jack was missing. It stretched before me like an invisible elastic band, ready to snap at any moment. The more I examined the key, the more certain I became that it would lead me to my brother. If only I could solve the riddle of who Jack had chosen as its temporary owner. I wasn't sure why – it was just a feeling I had.

Carefully, I put the key back beneath the flamingo lid, and slid the box into my pocket. I had no idea who S.F. was, but I had to make it my mission to find out.

Four

'It's only ten months,' Jack said as he was packing his rucksack one night in late September. He'd been working double shifts at Sutty's shop since his exams ended in June, to save enough money for going away. 'In fact, it's less than that. I've worked out that it's exactly 294 days until I come back. Look – I've scanned in a copy of my return flight so you can pin it on your noticeboard. And who knows, if you're lucky, Dad might fork out for a flight so you guys can come and see me in the Easter holidays. Wouldn't that be ace?'

Dad was on better terms with Jack since his A-level results, so it was possible that he might pay for us to visit him. I was keeping everything crossed that he would.

But somewhere, beneath the excitement surrounding Jack's trip, I knew that it was the end of how things used to be. He would return from his travels and then he'd go to uni and only be home in the holidays, and after that... well... he would probably move out for good. The thought of it made me so sad that I put it away in a locked chest in my mind and refused to open it again for a very long time.

I pictured myself at Jack's age and the choices I might make. I decided that if I took a gap year after finishing school, I probably wouldn't go travelling. Instead, I would spend time writing, without anyone disturbing me. I would start with my collection of riddle tales and later, maybe, I would write a whole book. I imagined finding a detective agency that might take me on as a part-time assistant, giving me real-life inspiration for my writing. Or working for a newspaper with a team of investigative journalists, provided they found me a spot on the crime desk.

I helped Jack fasten his backpack and checked under his bed to make sure he hadn't forgotten anything, while he drew a mini countdown of dates for me.

'Look,' he said proudly, 'every day you tick off means I'll be a day closer to home again.' And this is what I focused on to stop my mind wandering too far into the scary future.

I'd been carefully ticking the dates off every morning, but today, the date of the earthquake, I called 'The Day That Everything Changed'.

I didn't go to school on Friday. I'd spent the night lying on Jack's bed, unable to fall asleep. So much had changed in the last twenty-four hours that I half expected the 10.15 p.m. to New York to no longer appear in the skylight, but there it was – bang on schedule. Seeing that tiny flashing light made the breath catch in my throat. What if Jack and I never sat here again watching it together? And then I thought about all the unsolved riddles, all the unspoken conversations, all the advice not given – of everything that wouldn't happen if Jack didn't come home. I hadn't even managed to tell him that I'd decided to become a writer. I felt sick.

In the middle of the night, I went down to get a glass of water from the kitchen. I found Mum sitting there alone. Smiling sadly, she beckoned me to her.

'I can't sleep either, pet,' she said, giving me a squeeze. 'The whole thing seems so surreal, doesn't it?'

'Yes, like it's happening to somebody else.' I'd had this feeling ever since coming home from school, and in a strange way, it was a relief to hear that Mum felt the same.

'Here,' said Mum, handing me a cup of herbal tea. 'We need to get some rest so that we can speak to the police tomorrow. That's all we can do for now.'

In the end, we fell asleep together beneath a heavy throw on the living-room sofa.

We were awoken next morning by Dad speaking on the phone to the Foreign and Commonwealth Office, giving them as much detail as we had on Jack's whereabouts. Then he tried to get in touch with the Peruvian police, but the phone lines were down.

We'd just managed to eat a slice of toast when a Detective Inspector Pickles came round – Dad had reported Jack missing the previous night. When I first heard Pickles' name, I thought how it would have made Jack laugh. He sounded like a comic book character. But it turned out that DI Pickles was as thorough as Sherlock Holmes. He sat down at the kitchen table with us, and scribbled in his pad as we talked. His questions seemed to be never-ending.

Who was Jack travelling with? He was on his own. 'A lone traveller.' When he put it that way, it made me wonder whether Jack had felt lonely. The thought made the drumming start in my head, and I had to get up and walk around the room to try to make it stop.

When had he last been in touch with us? He'd FaceTimed Mum the previous week on Thursday, and he'd left Dad a voicemail on Monday. He'd sent me a text on Tuesday morning. Pickles wanted to see the message. I wished I hadn't told him about it, but Dad threw me a look and I handed over my phone.

How you doing, Flick? it said, *I'm heading to an awesome town called Arequipa. So many llamas here. Maybe I'll bring you one back if they let me smuggle him (or her) on the plane x*

Pickles raised his eyebrow and jotted something down. I tried to lean over to see what he was writing, but he angled his notebook away from me.

Did he post anything on social media that might have given a clue as to his whereabouts? Jack wasn't a regular poster, and his WiFi access had been unreliable for some of his journey. His last post on Facebook asked for hostel recommendations in Cusco, and his last photo on Instagram showed Jack in Arequipa, sandwiched between two volcanoes in the background. He looked thin, tanned and very happy. I gave Pickles the details of his accounts.

What were Jack's distinguishing characteristics? His blood, which wouldn't clot – although this wasn't something that anyone would know if they saw him. Mum told Pickles about his special medical kit which he carried at all times. It included his injections and a note from his doctor about what steps he, or those around him, must take if an accident occurred, causing Jack to lose blood quickly. Just saying that aloud made her panic even more.

Had he travelled alone before? No.

And so on. He was making us so nervous. I was desperate for him to leave. But when he finally did, things got even worse.

Dad tried to occupy himself by unloading the dishwasher, but his hands were shaking and he dropped one of Mum's favourite mugs. It was only a cheesy one with a cartoon superwoman on it that Jack had given her for Mother's Day a couple of years ago, but when the handle came off Mum burst into tears.

Dad went to hug her close. For a few moments, he held Mum as her shoulders trembled.

'I'm sorry,' he whispered and I didn't think he was talking about the mug. 'They're doing everything they possibly can, Gina. You know they are. And as soon as the power is up, they'll get on to the guys in Peru. He *will* be found.'

I took the glue from the kitchen drawer and busied myself with sticking the handle back on to the mug. The trick was to keep occupied.

The earthquake was constantly on the news. There was one photo that appeared over and over of a bridge in Lima. It looked as though a huge hand had grasped it in the middle, knuckles brushing the water, crumbling the middle section, squashing tiny cars with its shocking force and causing trucks to slide helplessly off the sides. It was horrific and yet strangely beautiful at the same time.

Even when the live coverage had stopped, there were hourly updates given by journalists in Peru and the UK. Usually the numbers rolled across the screen.

Number evacuated. Number injured. Number dead.

I started avoiding the living room so that I didn't have to see or hear the news. Whenever I needed to get to the front door from upstairs, I hummed as loudly as I could to block out the reports.

The one thing I did do was look up earthquakes online.

An earthquake is a shaking of the surface of the earth, resulting in the sudden release of energy in its upper layers.

It didn't tell me much. What I wanted to know was what Jack would have *felt*. How terrified would he have been? I read about the different earthquake magnitudes, ranging from almost unnoticeable to devastating, and learned that Jack's earthquake was towards the higher end of the scale. A lot depended on how far you were from the epicentre. The further, the better. The epicentre in this case had been near the capital, Lima, where Jack was heading to from Arequipa. But how far had he managed to get?

I searched further, skimming through more and more websites. What did it feel like to be in the middle of an earthquake? Survivors of large city-destroying quakes described them as 'huge bumps followed by a rolling and a shaking feeling', which somehow seemed inadequate. I shut my eyes, but I still couldn't imagine anything close. Then I found an article by a girl a little older than me, who'd said an earthquake felt as if a giant had picked up her house and given it a good shake, which was exactly my thought as I'd watched the bridge on TV. Words like 'unexpected', 'terrifying' and 'aftershock' jumped from the screen.

All this research made my head swim. I finally turned off the computer and rang Keira. Yesterday afternoon I'd sent her a message saying, *My brother is missing*. Even as I wrote it, it didn't seem real. She'd wanted to come over after school, but I hadn't felt like seeing anyone.

But now I needed to be with her. Plus, I wanted to tell her about the key and ask for her help in solving Jack's riddle.

'Oh Flick. It's horrid. I'm really, really sorry this has happened,' said Keira. This was why she was my best friend – unlike everyone else she didn't try to reassure me. She sat next to me and hugged me tight.

'S.F.? They're somebody's initials, right?' she asked when I told her about my discovery. 'But why would Jack leave this key in a box under his bed? Do you know what it's for? Does it open something, like a safe?'

'No, I don't think the key opens anything. It's just a piece of jewellery. Jack used to wear it around his neck, but he didn't take it with him, which is weird.' It struck me that it *might* open something, but if it did, Jack had never mentioned it to me, and now I had no way of finding out.

'Perhaps he was worried it would get lost while he was travelling? My mum always leaves her rings at home whenever we go on holiday.'

'Maybe. He keeps his most important stuff under the bed. I didn't see it when I was helping him pack before he left. He must have put it there at the last minute.'

'Well, for whatever reason, it's for S.F.'

'But I have no idea who that is. We need to find out.'

Keira racked her brains.

'I can think of a couple of people whose first names begin with S, but none of them have a surname with an F. Could you ask your parents?'

'I could, but they're in such a state, they probably won't even hear me.'

'Yeah, fair enough. Hey, it was your dad's fiftieth birthday a couple of months ago, wasn't it? Do you think your mum might have kept the invitation list?'

'Maybe. It's somewhere to start.'

I sneaked into the spare room, where I knew Mum kept her special gold-covered notebook and took it back to my bedroom. We scanned the guest list.

There were only three names that began with S – my aunts, Scarlett and Sally, and Sadie, from Dad's chambers. None of their surnames began with F.

'Think harder, Flick,' said Jack's voice in my head.

'Wait a minute,' I told Keira. 'I'll be back.'

In the second drawer of the spare room bedside table Mum kept her old address book, which she still used every Christmas for writing cards. I'd always found this funny for a person who ran a social media marketing company and had her life stored on her phone.

I turned the worn pages until I got to 'F'. I knew that she had all her contacts arranged by surname. There were only two entries – the first was Mum's old school friend, Emily Finnegan, but the second was Sol Falcon.

'Bingo,' said Keira. 'Who is he?'

'No idea.'

'Hmmm, it's unlikely, but let me check in case he's famous. Remember, your mum said she had some celebs that her agency represented.' She did a quick search on her phone, but shook her head.

'I think we need to do a search diagram,' I said.

'What's that?'

'You know, like a big spider diagram that detectives use to solve cases. Whenever we get a clue about an S.F. we can add it in.'

'Good plan. You want to do it on your noticeboard? Can we take some of these cards down?' she asked, indicating the pin board above my desk.

'No, I have the perfect place for it.' I told Keira to bring my Polaroid camera and the envelope of photos I'd taken on our last family holiday. Then we went up to Jack's room. The wall opposite his bed was covered in slippery whiteboard paper. He'd used the space to jot down ideas for his riddles and jokes – then he'd copy the best ones into his scrapbook. He'd wiped the wall clean before he left, as if it was a new start. Only faint outlines of his old drawings could be seen if I peered at them carefully.

'Could you search through that envelope and find a photo of Jack?' I asked Keira. I couldn't bear to look at any pictures of when we'd been so happy as a family.

Then I opened the flamingo box and took a close-up of the key.

'There aren't really any headshots. This is the closest I can find,' Keira said, passing me a photo of Jack squinting into the sunshine as he ate an ice cream. Mum had taken it as we walked down a coastal path in the South of France. It was a wonderful, hot day, which couldn't have been more different to today.

Jack's photo was our first item on the search diagram, followed by the key.

I decided that rather than making our diagram spider-shaped, I would draw a tree. Jack and the key would form its roots, and different branches would grow out of the trunk, each representing a different S.F. I drew a little lock at the end of every branch.

'I like what you've done,' said Keira. 'Now we need to find which of these locks the key fits.'

The way she said this sounded like one of Jack's riddles, which weirdly made me feel slightly better.

I took one of Jack's thick green markers and next to the first lock, wrote, 'Sol Falcon?' It wasn't much, but it was a start.

'I need to run,' said Keira. 'I'll keep thinking of other potential S.Fs. We'll solve this, Flick, I promise,' she said, giving me a big hug.

When she left, a strange quiet had descended on the house, and I realised that Mum had finally switched off the TV. I went downstairs to find her sitting in exactly the same position on the sofa, her knees tucked under her chin, staring into space. She looked like a tiny, frightened bird.

I sat next to her and stuck my head under her armpit, as I'd always done when I was little.

'Oh, hi, pet.'

'Hi. You OK, Mum?'

She looked at me with her lips pressed tightly together, trying not to cry, and then she slowly shook her head and hugged me. The screen of her work phone continued to light up with people trying to call her. She ignored them. She was only focused on her personal phone. I guessed that she'd given the number of this one to the police and the ICO.

'Not really, darling. I can't sleep,' she said. 'How have you been feeling? I should have asked earlier. I'm sorry. I realise I've been in my own world. It's horrible not being able to do anything. It gives you too much time to think.'

'Yeah, it's true. I'm OK though. Well, as much as I can be.'

'It's fine if you're not, you know. It's the most awful thing. I keep telling myself that they're doing everything they can to find him.'

'Yeah, everyone says that.'

'It doesn't help, eh?' Mum asked, rolling her eyes. It was the same expression that she used when Dad said something silly or when we found Auntie Chrissy's Instagram photos of her dog wearing a waistcoat. Only this time it was about Jack, and it made the tiny drummer start in my head again.

'Have there... have there been any updates?'

'Nothing. The police said that we'll be the first to know if they hear anything.'

She stared nervously at the two phones laid out on the coffee table. I noticed that she'd started picking the skin on her fingers. There were red tracks down the side of two fingernails on her right hand. The sight of them made me want to get her plasters, but I knew she'd be embarrassed by me noticing.

'Mum… Who's Sol?'

'Who?'

'Sol Falcon.'

'Do you mean Simon's dad?' I could see her lower lip begin to tremble. Simon was Jack's friend from school, who was supposed to be joining him in Peru. He hadn't saved enough money to do the whole trip with Jack, but he'd been due to fly out this coming weekend. He'd rung yesterday to say how worried he was and to ask if we'd let him know when we had news.

'Oh, yes.' I'd completely forgotten that Falcon was Simon's surname.

'Why do you ask?'

'No reason. I saw it written down somewhere,' I said, hoping that Mum wouldn't be suspicious. I don't know why I didn't tell her but something told me this was a puzzle I needed to work out on my own.

She didn't ask any more questions. Instead, she patted my hand.

'I'm going to have a shower now, pet,' she said quietly. She lifted herself carefully from the sofa and was gone before I could ask any more questions.

Simon... It took me a moment to register that I'd scored double points on Jack's puzzle already. I'd managed to find not one, but two people with the initials S.F. Simon was such an obvious answer to the riddle. He was one of Jack's newer friends – they'd only begun hanging out in their last year of school and they played tennis at the local club. After their A-level results came through, they started properly planning their gap year. Simon had already been to Brazil, so he didn't mind missing the first part of the trip. I remembered them looking at a huge map of South America on our living-room floor and excitedly drawing their route with a red pen. I wondered if he was still stacking shelves at Sutty's shop, where he and Jack had worked together through the summer.

I rang Keira to tell her what I'd learned.

'Why would he give the key to somebody who

was going on the same trip as him? That's the puzzling part. But you should go and speak to him anyway,' she said. 'Find out if he still works at Sutty's and if he does, ask to have a chat when he's on his break. Let me know what happens.'

She was right. I would go and speak to him tomorrow.

'The sooner, the better,' said Jack's voice in my head.

When I lay in bed that night, sleep didn't come. Instead, I thought of questions to ask Simon, or any other S.F. I could track down. I knew from the advice Jack had given me over the years that the main thing was to be discreet. I couldn't launch into asking whether they knew anything about the key.

After what felt like hours of brainstorming in the dark, I came up with these questions:

- Could you tell me three things about Jack that I might not know?
- Have you ever solved one of his puzzles?
- Do you know anything about a special item that he owned?

I couldn't reel them off as if I were conducting an interview. They would have to be cunningly slotted into casual conversation, which was easier said than done.

If I thought their answers were good enough, I would subtly introduce the subject of the key.

Finally, around 3 a.m. I fell asleep. I dreamed of Lady Abigail, walking along the dark lanes of Victorian London, calling 'Margot! Margot!' Her name echoed among the stone walls, returning fruitlessly to her mother's ears. But in those last moments before the sound dissolved into the night, it seemed to merge with Jack's name and the two danced together on a gust of wind.

Five

The first time Jack took me to Sutty's shop was a week after it had opened. He collected me from school and we took a detour on the way home, because he said he was craving chocolate. I suspected something straight away, because he hates sweet things, apart from that particular brand of American chocolate frog which Dad once brought back from a law conference in Boston, and which Jack had been buying from Sutty's ever since.

From the outside, Sutty's looked like an ordinary grocery shop, but inside, we found that it was anything but.

For starters, Sutty greeted each of his customers as though they were a long-lost friend. When he'd first opened his shop, he insisted on giving everyone a handshake, until some customers became a bit freaked out by his affection. He would settle for an excited wave from behind the till.

The second unusual thing was that every nook and cranny was rammed with stuff. Sutty's had shelves that towered to the ceiling, overflowing with all of the normal things you would find in a corner shop – milk, washing-up liquid, biscuits… and so much more. Indian silk fabrics spilled from woven baskets; there were dog beds with leopard print lining; fishing rods hung from the ceiling, along with headphones, strings of fairy lights and even feather boas, all forming an upside-down maze for taller shoppers. I loved it the moment I stepped through the doors and I could see why Jack wanted to show it to me.

'You're back,' said Sutty when we'd come in that day. 'Here for the goods, as agreed?' he asked winking. He emerged from behind the counter with a plastic cylinder filled with balls.

'Tennis balls?' I asked, confused.

'Ah, not just any tennis balls, my lady,' said

Sutty, 'they're glow-in-the-dark tennis balls. Your games will never be the same again.'

It seemed an odd thing to buy, even for Jack, who loved tennis. But as he never played late in the evening, and the courts in our local park had fancy floodlights, you could see everything, even in the dark. I was convinced that the balls were to be used as part of a joke and I vowed to ask Jack as soon as we left the shop.

'I played with them last week,' said a voice behind us, 'it's like hitting balls of fire.'

I turned around to see a tall, pale girl of about Jack's age with jet-black hair. She was wearing an oversized leather jacket and what looked like men's jeans. Her left eyebrow was raised in a mocking expression.

I glanced at Jack and for the first time ever, I saw his cheeks flush. He ran his hand over his face trying to hide it, but I could tell that the girl had noticed the effect she'd had on him.

'Manfy,' she said. 'Nice to meet you.'

'Jack.'

I looked from one to the other, wondering

what was going on, but neither of them gave anything away.

I was almost at the front door of Sutty's shop, when somebody called my name. I turned around and saw Duncan standing outside the bakery next door. Without his immaculate school uniform, he looked younger and friendlier.

'Hi. What are you doing here?' I asked him.

'Oh... Erm, my mom sent me out for some breakfast things... Mr Rox told us about your brother. I'm really sorry. I hope he gets found as soon as possible. If you need anything, you know, like any lesson notes for stuff that you miss, let me know. I'm good at taking notes.'

'Thanks,' I said, staring at Duncan with surprise. 'But I'll probably be back on Monday.'

I couldn't help but notice that he kept casting quick glances right and left, as if to make sure that nobody had seen him talking to me. It seemed that even in his moment of kindness, he was thinking about looking good.

I watched him cross the road, with his perfect posture and confident stride.

Luckily, I was spared from having to worry about this strange encounter any longer, because just then the door to Sutty's swung open and there he was.

'I'm deeply, deeply sorry,' he said simply. 'I've been watching it all on television. I keep hoping somebody will announce Jack is OK.' And then, strangely for him, he appeared lost for words.

'Thank you,' I said, although the drumming in my head was already rising in volume. 'I... I'm actually here to see Simon.'

'Ah, he's not here today. In fact he officially finished working here last week, but now that his... now that his plans have changed, I've told him that he could come back if he wanted to. He's going to do a stocktake for me on Monday...' Sutty began to explain but I felt my eyes blurring. I sat down on the front step. My shoulders shook.

I felt a big hand patting my back and then Sutty sat beside me, his huge body blocking the entrance to the shop. Luckily as it was early on a Saturday morning, there didn't seem to be any customers around.

We sat in silence and I rested my head on my knees to stop Sutty seeing me cry. I couldn't believe that Simon wasn't there. Monday was two whole days away. How would I fill that time? I wouldn't be able to dodge Mum and Dad, or avoid the drone of the TV news for another forty-eight hours.

From my strange position, all I could see was the edge of Sutty's frayed trouser leg and a small rectangle of the lower part of the open door which I bet nobody had ever looked at. It said, 'Sutantu Faasil and Sons'. My heart sped up. *S.F.*

'Is that you?' I asked, startling Sutty. His dark, bushy eyebrows shot up.

'What's me?'

'That,' I repeated, pointing to the sign. 'Is that your full name?'

'Oh! Yes, that's me for sure. Unless I've stolen someone else's shop.' He laughed, and then stopped, maybe thinking it was inappropriate in the circumstances.

Could it be possible that the key was meant for Sutty? I would never have guessed it, but then, as I'd learned from Jack, the answers to riddles often came from the most unlikely places.

'Do you mind if I ask you a few questions?'

'Anything,' he said, wiping his beard with his hand.

'Can you tell me about when you first met my brother?'

'Ah,' he said, and I noticed a grin playing across his lips. 'Now, that is a question that requires a long answer. Tell you what, wait here.' And for such a tall man, he jumped up quickly and was back moments later with his huge, green rain mac.

'I've asked Miranda to look after the shop. I think I'm due an early lunch. I've been working extremely hard today,' he said, winking at me and pulling me to my feet.

He took me to the greasy spoon cafe across the road.

'They do great hot chocolate in here,' he said. 'Do you want one? You can even have a shot of mint.'

We parked ourselves next to the misted-up window. A small child must have sat there recently, because outlines of handprints and crooked letters were scrawled on the glass. I had an image of Jack playing noughts and crosses with me on the window of the car on the way to France.

'You want me to tell you about when I met Jack?' I liked the way that he said Jack's name, the 'k' short and snappy, almost a clicking sound.

'Yes, exactly. Thank you.'

'It was when the shop first opened. My cousin arrived with a big delivery and we were unpacking boxes all day. Your brother turned up on his skateboard and said that he would help us out.'

'He just turned up?'

'Out of the blue, yes. A happy coincidence of the right person in the right place at the right time. He spent the rest of the day unloading stuff with me. It was more than sixty boxes. I offered to pay him of course – I'm not one to get people to work for free, oh no. But he wouldn't take any money. Nothing at all. He said he enjoyed it and it was his way of saying "welcome to the hood".'

I had no idea that Jack had done that for Sutty.

'He was looking at that same sign on the door – the one that says "Sutantu Faasil and Sons" and he came up with a great riddle. It went, "Tell me a sentence in which the word 'and' is used five times consecutively and it still makes grammatical sense". Do you know the answer?'

I mulled it over as Sutty went to collect our drinks. It was a strange riddle for Jack. I'd always thought he was terrible at grammar.

'I didn't know either,' he said, looking at my expression. 'It seemed impossible. But he told me eventually. Imagine you had a sign-maker who made that sign for you. You'd paid some decent money for it, but they managed to mess up the spacing between the words. So you'd have to tell them, "You didn't leave enough space between 'Faasil' and 'and', and 'and' and 'Sons'."

'We talked about all sorts that day,' Sutty continued. 'He asked about my family back home, so I told him about growing up in the Punjab. Then he told me about his sixth form trip to Kerala in India and the amazing experience he'd had there.

He'd felt inspired to travel the world. But there were so many countries on his list, you see, and I don't know which one came highest. Then he started to talk about his plans for his gap year...' Sutty trailed off and coughed awkwardly.

'Anyway, the second time we met was a day that I will carry with me for ever. It was the day that those horrible boys tried to steal Mick Morgan's wallet.'

The tiny drummer began beating his insistent rhythm. I couldn't bear to hear about Jack getting into trouble.

'They attacked him just after he left the shop. Two of them, probably in their twenties, although you couldn't tell because they had their hoods up. I hadn't even seen them come in. Mr Morgan always pops in late for his milk and bread, usually as we're about to close. I think he forgets to buy the essentials he needs. His dementia is getting bad. They got him on the side of the road, just there,' he said, pointing out of the window.

'I was about to run out, but I had a customer and in truth, I was scared. You never can tell with these people. They might have had weapons. I'm ashamed to say I got out my phone to call the police instead. But then I saw Jack come from across the road with Simon. They were heading back from tennis when they saw what was going on. It was amazing – they were onto those thugs in seconds. Jack pinned one of them to the floor. He didn't shout, but I could see that he was saying something to him. Then I saw the other one hand back Mr Morgan's wallet. I couldn't believe it – then they legged it.

'The poor man was shaking and they led him back into the shop to recover. The police arrived and Jack gave a statement. I hope it led to those idiots being caught. He's a brave man, your brother. And he has a calm way about him. His voice makes you stop and listen.'

'Jack? Jack and his friend helped Mr Morgan get his wallet back?'

I still couldn't process what Sutty was saying. It felt as if I was listening to a story about a stranger.

'Absolutely. I asked him what he'd said to the attackers to make them give back the wallet, but he wouldn't tell me. But you must know this whole story already?'

'No. He never told me,' I mumbled. I'd been certain that Jack told me everything, and included me in all of his secrets and plans, but it seemed this wasn't true. I wondered if he'd told Mum and Dad, but I doubted it. It was the sort of thing that Dad would have had a strong opinion about. Either he would have been incredibly proud or mad at Jack for taking the law into his own hands.

Without me even having to ask, Sutty had answered my first and second question, so the only thing left was to lead him to the final one. I wasn't sure how to drop it subtly into conversation as I'd intended, so I decided to come straight out with it.

'Do you know anything about a pendant that Jack used to wear?' I asked Sutty.

'A pendant?' he asked, not understanding.

'Like a necklace.'

He shook his head. 'I didn't realise he wore a necklace. Why do you ask?'

I looked into Sutty's deep brown eyes, and I could see that everything he'd told me was the truth. I also knew that he wasn't the one the key was meant for. But maybe he could be trusted to help?

'He left a pendant with a key on it meant for somebody with the initials S.F. and I'm trying to find them.'

'S.F? Wow. That's why you wanted to speak to me, eh?'

'You're the only person I've found with those initials, other than Simon.'

'Ah yes, Simon. Well they were – are – great friends, so you should speak to him. He is very likely the person it is meant for, no? Unless it could be Manfy?'

'Manfy?' I asked, not understanding, and then I recalled the girl we'd met at Sutty's shop the first day I went in with Jack.

'Her full name is Samantha. I can't think if her surname begins with an "F" but it is worth a try, no? Your brother liked her very much, and he helped her get a job when she was struggling.'

'Really? How do you know that?' I asked. My head felt as if it was about to burst with all the new information I'd found out about Jack in the last half an hour.

'She's a regular customer. She was so excited when she came in to tell me about it. She works at Gilmore's down the road. I remember now, she's Samantha Fabri – she has an unusual surname. You must speak to her.'

'Gilmore's? The estate agent?' Uncle Michael, Dad's brother, had been running Gilmore's since I was a baby. Would Jack have asked him to give this girl a job? It sounded so unlikely that I couldn't quite believe it.

'I'd better head back,' said Sutty, checking his watch, 'but you could always go and speak to her? She's a nice girl. She will be worrying about your brother too.'

I followed him out of the cafe in a daze, and slowly began to make my way home. Around me, the world had taken on a grey hue and the streets that I'd walked down thousands of times seemed somehow unfamiliar. I told myself that I was being silly – it was only the rain clouds gathering, casting everything into semi-darkness. But deep down I knew it came from something locked deep inside the treasure chest of my thoughts – the realisation that perhaps I didn't know Jack as well as I thought.

Six

'Your brother and Simon battled two thugs to get an old man's wallet back?' asked Keira, her dark eyes widening.

'That's what Sutty said.'

I had told her the whole story from start to finish.

'And he managed to get this girl a job with your uncle?'

'Yep.'

'And you never heard about any of this?'

Keira had known Jack almost as long as she'd known me. Our parents were good friends and she was always staying over – it was pretty much her second home. She knew the full story of Jack's detentions and his arguments with my dad.

'No, never.'

'Well, at least we've got a lead in our case. We need to speak to this girl, Manfy, don't we?'

'Yeah, but how? We can't just go in there and talk to her. The only time I met her, I got the impression that she was much more interested in Jack than me.'

'We could go undercover?'

'D'you think she'll believe that we're going to buy a house? She's not stupid.'

'I meant more like hanging around outside and waiting until she goes on her break. It's Saturday. Most estate agents are still open, aren't they? Let me check Gilmore's website.'

She brought the details up on her phone and gave me a thumbs up. 'Open until 4 p.m. There's a good chance she's working. We could at least try. Come on.'

'I suppose, but isn't that a bit weird? What would we do? Hang outside?'

'It's on the high street so we could look in the shops next door and keep half an eye on their front door.'

I didn't have any better ideas, so in the end I agreed with Keira. We spent half an hour pottering around the card shop, making the owner increasingly suspicious, and then we walked up and down the high street several times, pretending to be window shopping. I was ready to give up and go home when Keira nudged me in the ribs. A car had pulled up outside Gilmore's. The driver, who was a woman, parked and stepped onto the pavement. She was wearing a pencil skirt and suit jacket.

'Is that her?' Keira whispered.

I shook my head, but then I looked closer and saw the dark hair and pale skin. I'd barely recognised Manfy without her leather jacket. She must have felt our gaze, because she turned and I could see a glimmer of recognition in her eyes.

'Flick?' she called over, and her face rearranged itself into a look of concern.

'How do you know my name?' I blurted out.

'Oh… We met before, didn't we? I have a good memory. And your brother told me a lot about you. Have you… have you had any news?'

'No, nothing yet,' I said. I was beginning to dread the question, and I guessed I would be hearing it repeated, over and over. I wondered if this had been a bad idea after all.

I must have had a pained expression on my face, because Manfy asked, 'Are you all right?'

'Actually, d'you mind if we come in to have a glass of water?' Keira asked her, linking her elbow through mine.

'Course,' said Manfy. 'I'm on a half day today and I've finished, so I can make you a cup of tea.'

This was only the second time that I'd been inside Gilmore's. The first was many years ago, when Uncle Michael had set up the agency and I'd gone along with Mum and Jack to take a look at the office. We'd gone for a trip to a cavernous furniture warehouse to get the place kitted out. The navy leather sofas that we'd chosen were still there – now looking very battered. I could still visualise Jack sitting on them in the shop, checking for 'bounce factor'. 'If you get the level of bounce right, then people will know that you mean business,' he'd told Uncle Michael, who had nodded seriously.

The place looked the same as it had back then. The only difference was that somebody had painted one of the walls bright blue, and on it, had drawn a huge, old-fashioned house with loads of windows, and pillars framing the front door. I paused before it, mesmerised. It was the kind of house that I imagined Lady Abigail and Margot living in. I could see them eating in the dining room with Henry, the servants busy at work in the kitchen, making bread for the following morning's breakfast.

I wanted to ask Uncle Michael who had painted the house, but he wasn't there. The only other person was a bored-looking young man with a goatee beard, who glanced at us before turning back to his screen. Manfy led us into the staffroom, which was tiny, with a round table, chairs and a shelf with a microwave and kettle. I noticed that the place was spotless and Manfy took great care in making the tea, even arranging a little fan of biscuits onto a plate.

'I'll be back in a sec. Going to get changed,' she said.

She disappeared into the loo with her rucksack and re-emerged a couple of minutes later resembling the girl I'd met at Sutty's – in ripped black jeans and a T-shirt with a skull on it.

She sat cross-legged on one of the chairs opposite us.

'I couldn't breathe when I first saw it on the news,' she said quietly. 'But that must be nothing compared to how you're feeling. I tried calling him straight away – bet you did too.'

I had. Fifty-three attempted calls so far. Fifty-three times I'd reached the recorded message in Jack's joking tone, 'What never asks questions but is always answered? Ha, that one's too easy. I'll try to answer the phone one day, promise. In the meantime, leave a message. Cheers.' I had lost hope of him answering. I just needed to hear his voice.

The drumming in my head began to build. It was an angry beat – fast and heavy. How dare this girl who I hardly knew have done exactly the same thing as me when she found out about Jack? I'd spent a lifetime with him – he was a part of my earliest memories, and his name, according to Mum, was the first word I'd said. Manfy had known him for what seemed like five minutes. My fists clenched and I had to sit on them to try to calm down.

'Sutty said that Jack helped you to get this job?' said Keira, glancing at me anxiously.

'Oh, he did a lot more than that,' she said. 'I was a right mess when he met me. I was pretending I wasn't, of course, but it was awful.'

She stopped talking and began fiddling with the leather strap on her key ring, as if embarrassed by the memory.

'Why was it so awful?' Keira asked insistently.

'I didn't have a job, or a place to live, and I had £12.45 in my pocket to last me for ever. I'd been trying to save it, so I'd been eating rice cakes for a week. There were these guys at the hostel I was staying at who were always fighting. I'd be woken in the middle of the night by people being beaten up and I knew I wouldn't be able to stay there for much longer. I felt as if I was drowning.'

I looked at her to see whether she was making this up. Jack always said I have a great knack for knowing if someone is lying, but she was deadly serious and looked me straight in the eye.

'Why were you homeless?' I found myself asking. My fury fell away and I was glad that I hadn't said anything.

'I'd had a massive row with my mum. We've never got on and we were always arguing. We lived in this tiny flat in Grimsby. She'd had it with me when I dropped out of college and then her boyfriend moved in. He's a nasty piece of work. The less I tell you about him, the better. Anyway, I couldn't stand it any more, so one day I took all the money that I had saved up – about a hundred pounds – and I caught a coach down to London.

'Mum didn't even call after I left and I didn't call her either. The trouble was that I didn't have a plan. I knew that I needed to get away. I got in touch with a friend's brother who owned a pub in Vauxhall. He said I could work there in return for a room upstairs, but when I turned up, well – let's say that things didn't work out on any level, and I was stuck.'

'Why didn't you go home?' Keira asked.

'I couldn't. One of the guys at the pub had found me this hostel and I kept trying to get work at the

Job Centre, but I had no qualifications, only my driver's licence. I managed to get an interview for a retail role, but in the end, they took on someone else who'd done it before. That was with Jamal, Sutty's brother. He did get me a couple of cleaning jobs at Sutty's which is where I first bumped into Jack.'

'I remember that day. I thought you were a customer. You seemed so – you know…'

'Confident? Chilled?'

'Yeah.'

'I'm a good actress. Your brother came after school the next day and found me in tears outside the shop after my shift. I was so hungry. He bought me fish and chips. I hadn't eaten a proper meal in days… Then he asked if I wanted to talk about whatever it was that had made me cry. I thought he was trying to chat me up but I ended up blurting it all out because I felt so lonely. We sat together on a wall on Kavanagh Street and I talked and talked.'

'And did he, you know – ask for your number?' asked Keira. I could tell by the tone of her voice that she was getting impatient. She was itching to get to the real questions that we wanted to ask.

'What? No. I mean he did, but not in *that* way. When I told him I was broke, he wanted to give me some money, but I refused. So he said that I should treat it as a loan, and I told him I had no job. Then he asked what sort of stuff I could do, and said that his uncle was looking for a receptionist. I thanked him, but I thought it was just chat. So when he messaged me a couple of days later to say that I had an interview the following week, I couldn't believe it. I ended up spending most of the money he'd lent me on a dress because I didn't have anything professional to wear. I've been here almost a year now. I'm in a nice flat-share too, because I could afford to move out of the hostel when I got my first payslip from Michael.'

'Do you like it here?' I asked. Now that she had changed back into her own clothes, I couldn't imagine Manfy working in an office.

'Yes. I used to be on reception, but last month I got promoted to a sales role. I get to drive around and show people properties. Some of them are huge, with swimming pools and everything. It's fun to imagine living in a house like that. Michael's a great boss and the money's not bad. I never imagined that

I'd be working in an estate agent's. I always thought I'd be a musician or a photographer. I still might be one day – I love taking pictures. You never know, do you?'

'What sort of photos do you take?'

'I have an old camera that belonged to my dad. It still uses film. I don't put my photos on Instagram or anything. I only have hard copies that are mine to keep. It makes them more special. I like taking photos of people, capturing what makes them unique. With Jack, it was the way he laughed – he almost completely closed his eyes. Did you ever notice that?'

'Of course,' I said, and I knew that my voice had an angry edge to it. I think Manfy heard it, because she put her hand on top of mine as if to show her support.

'I've taken a couple of good shots of him. I'll give them to you when I develop the film,' she promised.

'Did you and Jack end up going out?' I asked, swallowing hard. I dreaded the answer, because if she said 'Yes', it would be another part of my brother's life that I knew nothing about.

'No,' she said and I could feel my shoulders

relaxing. 'But we hung out together a lot. I offered to teach him guitar in return for everything he'd done for me. He was getting good by the end – I mean, before he left.'

I recalled the battered guitar that Jack had bought second-hand from a music shop near Tottenham Court Road. He used to strum it sometimes when we sat in his room and chatted.

'He was talking about doing grades, because his music teacher at sixth form had encouraged him. He sounded like a pretty awesome guy from what Jack said. Nothing like the teachers I had – they really didn't seem to care at all.'

'What was his name?' Keira asked.

'Who?'

'This teacher?'

'Oh, Finny. I'm pretty sure it's a nickname – it's what Jack used to call him. Finny taught him how to read music. I only taught myself the different strings. I don't actually know any notes.'

'So you would hang out and play the guitar?' It was only when I said it aloud that I realised that I was jealous. I knew how stupid that was, but I couldn't help it. He was totally allowed to have this other part of his life. We'd still done loads together.

'Yeah, and sometimes at the shop. He was such good fun,' Manfy continued. I hated that she kept using the past tense. 'Did he ever tell you about the trick we played on Sutty?'

I shook my head.

'Sutty is petrified of ghosts. He kept telling us about how his parents' house is haunted. Unexplained things went on there, like stuff going missing and glasses getting smashed in the middle of the night. His mum dismissed all these things as random accidents but Sutty was sure there were supernatural forces at play.

'Anyway, he used to do stocktakes at the shop once a month, usually on a Friday evening, and he would pay me and Jack to help. On one of those evenings, Jack thought it would be hilarious to pretend to go to the loo, fiddle with the fuse and turn all the lights off. Then he put an old white sheet over one of the kids' toy drones that Sutty sold – the ones operated by a remote control – and sent it flying round the shop, banging into walls and shelves, causing loads of stuff to fall down. He played some shrieking sounds that he'd found on a YouTube horror film clip to make it even scarier.

'I couldn't stop laughing – it looked so ridiculous, but Sutty was scared out of his mind.'

The thought of Jack's 'ghost' whizzing round the shop was enough to make even me smile. I noticed that the horrible drumming in my head had eased as Manfy was talking and, as I drank my sugary tea, I began to feel a bit better.

'He loves a practical joke,' I said.

'Did he tell you the one that he played on your grandma?'

'On Grandma Sylvie?' I couldn't believe that anyone would dare play a joke on her. She had always been super-strict, even with her appearance: she had flawless make-up, poker straight hair, and her immaculately plucked eyebrows disappeared into her fringe when she was cross. Then you knew you were in Deep Trouble.

'Yeah, it was a great one,' Manfy continued. 'She was mad for a while, but she forgave him in the end. How could you not forgive Jack?'

Manfy's story was interrupted by an urgent beeping from her phone.

'I totally forgot I was supposed to be collecting the keys from my new landlord,' she said, wincing. 'But here, take my number,' she added, scrawling it on a piece of paper and handing it to me hastily. 'Please, please could you let me know if you hear anything about Jack?'

'Sure. I'll let you know as soon as I hear anything,' I promised.

'Well, that was useless,' I said, as Keira and I walked home. She'd taken the piece of paper from me and was punching Manfy's number into her phone. 'All we managed to find out was that she used to hang out with Jack, apparently much more than I ever did. Plus we didn't even ask her if she knew anything about the key.'

I realised how sulky I sounded, but I didn't care. If Jack had kept so much of himself hidden from me, what was the point of carrying on with his riddle? I might never find the answer.

'I'm guessing you missed the two potential S.F.s that were given as clues?'

'Eh?'

'Come on, I thought that Jack had trained you well? She gave away some very important information, Flick. The first was Finny, the music teacher. That's Mr Finnegan from school, isn't it? My cousin had him last year for her A-levels. We can easily look up his first name on the school website. I have a suspicion it begins with an "S". The second is your grandma, isn't it?'

I was so surprised that I stopped dead in my tracks. 'She's also an S.F, isn't she? Sylvie Florenz.' It sounds silly but I'd completely forgotten her full name. To me, she was always Grandma.

'Exactly,' she said. 'So…'

'So?'

'Who shall we visit first?'

 # Seven

I spent most of Sunday morning sitting in Jack's room sketching the house that I saw on the wall at Gilmore's and thinking of both Margot and Jack. I couldn't feel mad at Jack for long. I loved to sit on his windowsill and watch the world from above. Our road was on a hill, and if I put my face against the glass and looked east, I could see the river and the majestic bridge that had been around for centuries. It was strangely calming to look at something that had remained the same when everything around it had changed. In the summer, the bridge was barely visible because the leaves on the trees obscured it so that I couldn't see the road below. This was Jack's favourite view.

'I can imagine that I'm anywhere in the world,' he said, 'on the French Riviera, or in the middle of the Amazon jungle. I wake up, see the light streaming in through the leaves and choose my location.'

Now the bare branches swayed in the breeze like skinny dancers. It had grown steadily colder over the past week and the weather forecast predicted snow. I wasn't getting my hopes up. Sleet and rain were much more likely. As if in answer to my thoughts, a smattering of raindrops hit Jack's windowpane. I was about to go downstairs when I spotted a girl wearing a red beret walking energetically down the street. She looked so much like Margot I couldn't take my eyes off her. She paused at the zebra crossing, tilting her head as if to feel the chill breeze on her face. I noticed that she was carrying a first aid kit – a little box with a cross on it. Perhaps she was a nurse? She looked up and caught me watching and waved. Embarrassed, I stepped back from the window, but realised I was being silly. When I put my hand up to wave back it was too late – she'd gone.

That evening Mum, Dad and I sat down together for dinner for the first time since the earthquake. We were eating our way through the provisions that friends and neighbours had made for us, and today Keira's mum's cottage pie was on the menu.

'I'm sorry I didn't manage to cook anything,' said Mum. 'I can't seem to focus on anything. Even chopping an onion seems like a difficult task.'

'It's all right, darling,' said Dad, and I was surprised to see him get out of his seat to give her a hug. 'I think we all know that the normal routine has fallen apart since we found out about Jack,' and he motioned with his left hand that I should join them.

This three-way hug made me feel safe, but there was also something not quite right about it – like we should be forming a square, not a triangle. There was a vital person missing.

'We need to support each other through this,' said Mum.

I desperately wished I knew what to say to make

us all feel better. Then the phone rang and our hug broke apart. It was Pickles.

Mum and Dad quickly took the phone into the study and shut the door behind them. Maybe they thought that they were protecting me from hearing any bad news but I needed to know too and decided to listen in through the wall.

'Nothing at all?' Dad asked. There was silence and his voice got louder. 'Of course we can't be certain that he was in the area, but the last time that we spoke to him he was heading there. We've told you this already. Yes, I know that you are – I'm not raising my voice, I understand that you're doing everything...'

Then I heard Mum burst into tears and I couldn't listen any longer. I sneaked upstairs, threw my pyjamas and toothbrush into my rucksack and ran outside.

When I knocked on Keira's front door, nobody answered. The living-room light was on, but the rest of the house was in darkness and I couldn't hear the classical music that her mum, Charlie, always played in the kitchen.

I fished my phone out of the bottom of my bag and saw a message from Keira that said: *Gone to visit Grandpa Miles. See you at school tomorrow! Xx*

I sat on her porch steps twisting my rucksack straps round and round my finger as I debated what to do.

In the left-hand hedge I felt for the small fish-shaped piece of slate that Charlie had put there when she and Keira had first moved in. Their spare front door key was kept underneath. I considered letting myself in and waiting for Keira in her room, surrounded by her old unicorn wallpaper and fairy lights. I could have sent Mum a message; she was so preoccupied she wouldn't have known there was nobody in next door. I was about to pick up the key when something brushed against my leg. A black and white smudge crossed my path and bolted in through the cat flap. I breathed out. It was only Gilbert, Keira's cat, who was surprisingly fast for his old age, and horribly grumpy. He'd known me for years, yet he would still hiss and claw at me if I dared to sit next to him on the sofa.

Spending any amount of time alone with Gilbert didn't seem so appealing. I thought of Keira with her mum and grandpa and I felt terribly lonely. Suddenly I knew what I needed to do – I would go for a very overdue visit to Grandma Sylvie's. And as she was one of the S.F.s that we'd identified, I would ask her about the key.

Her house was only a ten-minute cycle ride away. Realising this made me feel guilty for not seeing her in so long. Over the past year, she'd become quite ill. It began with pains in her knees, and then her arthritis got so bad that she couldn't leave the house. Eventually she couldn't get out of bed without help. Now, Mum visits Grandma every other day, often with some new medication to help ease the pain in her poor legs. I think she wishes she could spend more time with her, and she's already cut down her days at work. For the days she's not around, she's found Grandma a nice French carer, who she's really pleased with. I used to see Grandma once a week with Jack, but recently, we'd gone less and less.

I went to collect my bike from the shed and messaged Mum to tell her my plans.

As I turned into Grandma's street, a memory resurfaced. I was about five years old and running down this same road with Jack. We were racing to our grandparents' door. He was pelting down the street, his trainers thudding on the pavement and I was giggling, desperately trying to catch up. When I thought he was miles ahead and that I'd never be able to shorten the distance, Jack slowed down, panting heavily. I saw my opportunity to overtake, using my last reserves of energy to run as fast as I could, and slammed the gate triumphantly. Jack had obviously let me win but I didn't think this at the time. He slapped me on the back to congratulate me. I tried to recall his exact words, but the memory was gone as quickly as it had come, and I found myself standing alone outside Grandma's glossy black door.

I rapped on the brass knocker before I could change my mind. I heard chatter in the hallway, someone laughing, and a tall lady with blonde hair pulled into a tight ponytail appeared at the door.

'Erm, hi,' I stuttered, 'I'm here to see my grandmother.'

The woman raised her eyebrows in surprise.

'Ah, you must be Felicity, no?' she asked, ushering me in. 'I am Gertrude.' She had a strong French accent and perfect make-up. I noticed the dark cat-eye flicks of eyeliner in the corners of her eyes. I wasn't sure what I'd imagined when Mum told me about getting Grandma a carer, but it wasn't this glamorous woman.

Grandma was born and raised in Quebec, the French part of Canada, although she'd lived in England for more than fifty years. Mum must have thought she'd like someone French to look after her, maybe to remind her of when she was young. I'm sure that Grandma approved of Gertrude's stylish appearance. She enjoyed looking good herself, even in her late seventies.

I followed Gertrude down the corridor. Nothing had changed in the months that I'd been away. Old black and white photographs of Grandma's French family lined the walls, the lights were dimmed and the place smelled of perfume and cigarettes, which she had never managed to give up, despite a recent incident with one of her rugs catching fire.

'*Qui est là?*'

'It's your granddaughter,' Gertrude replied, beckoning me into the living room, where Grandma sat on the sofa in her silk dressing gown, her legs propped on a footstool. She coughed with confusion at seeing me.

'Felicity? What are you doing here? Is there any update on Jack?' I'd never seen her look so worried. Grandma could be disapproving, stern, sometimes angry, but never worried.

'No, nothing new,' I told her quickly. 'I've just come to visit.'

'Visit?' Grandma echoed.

'Please, sit down,' Gertrude said, motioning towards the wicker rocking-chair that Jack always sat in when we'd come here together. I avoided it, perching instead on the edge of the sofa, opposite Grandma.

'Have you had dinner?' asked Gertrude, looking at me, concerned. 'We have some tomato soup left, or perhaps you may like some *gougères*?'

I was about to protest that I'd already eaten, but in reality I'd barely touched my food before running out of the house. Also, hearing the word '*gougères*' made me change my mind. I hadn't had them in a long time, but if I shut my eyes, I could still taste the glorious, melt-in-the-mouth French pastry. I once tried to describe to Keira what they were, eventually settling on 'little clouds from cheese heaven'. The strange thing was that Grandma was normally a terrible cook. These were the only things that she made which were not only edible, but delicious. When Jack was my age now, he could easily eat five of them at once, even if it meant that he felt sick on the way home.

'Yes, thank you,' I found myself saying.

'And if you could bring us some tea, please,' Grandma said. 'In the nice navy blue tea set.'

She was bringing out her finest china for me. I felt doubly guilty that she saw my visit as such a rare and special occasion.

'Her *gougères* are even better than mine,' she whispered when Gertrude had gone into the kitchen. 'Your mother did very well finding her. How is she doing?'

'Mum? Not terrible,' I lied, 'but obviously worried. How are you? How are your legs?'

'Oh,' she said, looking down at them as if she'd completely forgotten about the pain. 'Doesn't matter about that…'

Grandma loved talking about her aches and pains. Jack and I could hardly get a word in edgeways whenever we'd come round. We loved counting the number of times she used her favourite phrases, which were 'ghastly' (to describe places which she disapproved of), 'tolerable' (about people she vaguely admired) and 'magnificent' (anything French, from food to music). Today she sat in silence and looked at me. Her grey eyes were sad and for the first time I felt as though we understood each other.

'Funnily enough, I was thinking about Jack as you came in,' she whispered. 'He never seems to leave my thoughts.'

'Same.'

'I close my eyes and imagine he's here,' she said, motioning to the wicker chair, 'playing that tune on the guitar – you know, the happy one? I forget who it's by. It's quite famous… He always played it to me when I felt particularly sad.'

'He played to you?'

I couldn't remember why I'd stopped visiting Grandma with Jack. When I'd started secondary school I began to make excuses, saying I needed to finish my homework or that I was doing something with Keira. Jack would offer to reschedule for a different time, but I told him there was no need. I didn't understand why he wanted to keep seeing her. She never seemed interested in what we were doing and she was so prim and proper. I was scared of putting a foot wrong when I was at her house. Mum always ignored Grandma's tutting and laughed if she made comments about her cooking or clothes, but I couldn't. It annoyed me too much.

'Oh, yes,' said Grandma. 'Every time he came. At first he wasn't great and he kept making mistakes, but he soon improved. He's a high achiever, your brother.'

'You never used to think that before,' I blurted out.

I clapped my hand over my mouth. I couldn't believe I'd said that aloud. I lowered my eyes waiting for Grandma to tell me to leave. But she sighed and said, 'Maybe I didn't say it enough. He's very talented. In fact, you're both intelligent. Only you're much more grounded – I feel as if you know what you want to do with your life. Am I right?'

'I want to be a writer,' I said hesitantly. I almost immediately regretted it, but I saw that Grandma looked impressed.

'A writer, eh? I'm sure you will be excellent. It's a job that demands imagination and perseverance, and I think you have both. I should be glad to read something of yours. Luckily, I still have my eyes, though my legs are useless. Will you show me your writing?'

'I'd like that.' I also liked that Grandma was using the present tense when talking about Jack. I loved her for it.

'I heard that Jack played a trick on you?'

Her eyes lit up.

At that point, Gertrude returned carrying a tray of tea and *gougères*. I took one and bit into the pastry as she put them on the table. Grandma had been right. They were even better than I remembered. For a moment I forgot the awfulness of everything that was happening, relishing the feather-light, cheesy wonder in my mouth.

'Yes, he did. Well, now that I think about it, perhaps he only wanted to make me feel good. It was a late Friday afternoon in early December. I woke up to something hitting my bedroom window. I looked outside, but there was nobody there. Just the empty street and this beautiful tune coming from somewhere in the distance – it was divine, so slow and soulful. I called out to see whether anybody would answer, but there was nobody there. When I was leaving to go to the shop the next day, I found a rose outside the front door. It was frozen by the time I rescued it, but it was obviously from the same person who had serenaded me.'

'And who did you think it was?' I asked her. I imagined Jack with his guitar, his parka fastened up tight against the cold, strumming his guitar in a hidden spot in Grandma's garden.

'I thought,' said Grandma, and she cleared her throat awkwardly, 'that it was Martin.'

'Martin?'

'Mr Percy.'

'Your gardener? You thought he was serenading you?'

'Well, yes. Don't look at me like that. I'm a stupid old woman to think that, I know. Truth be told, I always thought he was a bit stuck-up. He seemed to think that there was nobody better when it came to understanding plants, but he always looked at me in this peculiar way, you know.'

'I know somebody exactly like that,' I said, thinking of Duncan.

'Really?' asked Grandma. I could see her cheeks glowing red beneath her blusher.

'You asked him, didn't you? You asked if it was him? Oh, Grandma!'

'I did. And naturally he denied everything. But... well...'

'What happened?' I demanded, seeing that there was more to it than she was letting on.

'He asked if I wished that it had been from him, and I told him not to be so ridiculous. But we spoke frankly for the first time in years, and he invited me to dinner. I wore my red dress – the one

I hadn't worn since your parents' wedding. It still fits, you know. We only went to the Italian place on the high street. It wasn't anything that special.'

'You went on a date?' I asked, amazed. I couldn't imagine Grandma in her red dress in a restaurant with the gardener. It sounded like something out of Cluedo.

'But how did you go all the way to the high street?' I looked at her legs stretched out, the knees swollen.

'I have a new electric wheelchair,' she told me. 'Your mum arranged it for me – it's very good of her. I just need to press a few buttons and I can go exactly where I want to. But sometimes Martin insists on pushing me. He's such a gentleman, you know.'

'Do you think that's what Jack wanted to do? To set the two of you up?'

'Quite possibly. He never admitted it though. He smiled at me in the way he always does – you know that cheeky half-smile he has?'

I knew it well. Only the left side of his mouth went up and a dimple appeared.

'Of course.'

'He certainly knows how to bring fun into people's lives, doesn't he? And you know what? I'm glad that he does. I was worried about him when he was little and we first found out about his illness. His doctor at the time seemed to think that Jack should avoid all risk and that he should be taken entirely out of harm's way. "Even a grazed knee might be dangerous," she said. I'm sure you know, but for ages he wasn't allowed to do loads of things.'

'I know.' When I'd insisted on going to a trampolining park for my sixth birthday Jack watched from the side, reading a book. He pretended that he was too old for bouncing madly up and down, but I could tell that he would have loved to have joined in if he could.

'I'm glad he didn't let haemophilia stop him,' said Grandma and I had to agree with her.

'Who knows what he'll do next?' she continued. 'Martin thinks that Jack will play in a band of some sort. You know teenagers these days are into forming bands? Then they get into drinking and all sorts of trouble. But deep down I don't think he's that kind of a musician. You can tell that he really enjoys playing to individual people, not huge crowds. I bet he would love to teach guitar. He definitely has a knack for it.'

I didn't know what to say. I stared at the TV where a black and white film was still running. Grandma must have turned off the sound when I'd arrived. On the screen, a band was playing on stage – two guitarists, a bass player and a singer. Before them, couples were rotating around the dance floor in time to the music. I wondered if it was soul, or blues or jazz.

I thought about all the different versions of Jack that I'd discovered since his disappearance: Jack the helper, the caring friend, the musician, the matchmaker. But the more I thought about it, the more I realised that they weren't new at all. They were versions that we didn't see at home. Or maybe that we didn't want to accept. I saw the exciting, daring older brother, and Mum and Dad saw the son who didn't seem to want to take the road that they'd mapped out for him.

When I'd first found out these new things about Jack, I'd felt cheated and a little bit sad. But there were things that Jack didn't know about me too. He had no idea how much I like writing as I'd never shared any of my stories with him. I wanted to perfect them – to make them as good as they could be before he read them. I wondered whether this was, in a way, what Jack had been doing too. Maybe he wasn't quite sure what he wanted to do with his life and he was waiting until he'd made a decision before he told us. Although he knew Keira, who was always round at our house, he didn't really know any of my other friends. So perhaps it wasn't so strange that I didn't know many of his.

Gertrude turned on the fire, and I crawled over to Jack's wicker chair, nestling in it. We sat in silence, watching the dancing couples on the screen. My eyes grew heavy.

Grandma's voice woke me up.

'Felicity, it's late. I'm going to ring your mother to say you'll stay here tonight. Gertrude, will you make up the bed in the spare room? Felicity can borrow one of my nightgowns.'

'I have some pyjamas with me,' I mumbled. 'I thought I was staying at Keira's but, well, here I am.'

Half an hour later, I was lying in a huge double bed in what Grandma called the Yellow Room, which had been Mum's room when she was little. Some of her old things were still here – the wooden house, home to a family of scary-looking dolls with oddly big heads, a pile of French storybooks and the postcards that Grandpa sent from all over the world when he travelled with the Navy. '*Ma petite souris*' he'd called her – 'my little mouse'.

At the top of the bed, there was a big photograph of Grandma and Grandpa when they were young, probably before Mum was born. They were standing in a valley, with green mountains towering above them and the outline of a river in the background. Grandpa was carrying a big backpack and they looked incredibly happy.

I curled up into a tight ball, breathing in the room's faint musty smell, and thought what a good idea it had been to come here.

Eight

It was Monday morning and I'd set Mum's old bedside alarm to 6.45 a.m. so that I had plenty of time to get home and change for school. As I was pulling on my jeans, I stepped up onto the bed and studied the picture again. I was trying to see how Grandad had looked when he was younger. I'd only been six when he died and Jack had been twelve. This young, smiling, blond man looked different to the grey-haired, stooping Grandpa I remembered, but there was definitely something about his eyes that was familiar. They were eyes which smiled, the corners creased up with kindness. I saw now that Jack had inherited those eyes.

Then I studied Grandma, who gazed at her husband adoringly. That was when I noticed it. In the photo she was dressed in a white shirt with an open collar, and she wore a fine gold chain around her neck. From the chain dangled a tiny key.

I felt lightheaded. I opened the curtains to let in the sunshine, examining the necklace from every angle. I took Jack's key from my pocket, held it up against the photo and compared the two. I was certain that they were the same key.

I ran down the stairs, still in my pyjamas.

'Grandma! Grandma!' I shouted. She was sitting at the kitchen table, wearing a silk dressing gown with a frilly collar and ruffled sleeves, of the exact kind that I imagined Lady Abigail would wear. She jumped in her seat as I came into the kitchen.

'What's happened?'

'Is this yours?' I asked her breathlessly, opening my palm to show her the key.

'Oh,' she said staring at it calmly, 'yes. Well, it used to be. I thought it was Jack's now…'

'Did you give it to him?'

'Yes, a few years ago. He found it lying in my old jewellery dish and asked about it. I saw how much it fascinated him, so I gave it to him since I hardly wore it any more.'

'Where is it from?' I asked her.

'Grandpa bought it for me when we were travelling on our honeymoon. It's from a little key factory in Peru.'

'In Peru?' I asked in disbelief. 'You've been to Peru? Is that where the photo upstairs was taken?'

'The one in the Yellow Room? That's from Patagonia in Chile,' said Grandma. 'Your grandfather travelled to Chile, Argentina and Peru with the Navy and told me wonderful things about South America. It made me want to go myself and I'm glad I did. Peru is the most fascinating country. I'm afraid that I told Jack all about it… I might have been the one who persuaded him to go there.'

Her voice began to shake, so I changed the subject.

'Grandma, do you think Jack would have left the key for you?' I asked her. 'I don't understand why he didn't take it with him. He used to wear it every day, but here it is, and there was a note with it that says he'd left it "For S.F."'

'For S.F?' Grandma asked, looking puzzled. I could sense straight away that the message meant nothing to her, but I thought it would be wise to double check.

'You don't think he meant you?'

'I don't think so, Felicity. We hadn't spoken about the key. I'm not sure why he would have wanted to give it back to me. Besides, if he did, don't you think he would have written "Grandma" instead of my initials?'

'I suppose,' I agreed. 'Is there anything else that you can tell me about the key?'

'Well, I'm not sure it's worth very much. I think it's made of iron. There were lots of them at this little market stall next to the key factory. The stall owner seemed a bit desperate to sell. He told us that the keys had magical powers. Apparently whoever bought one would be granted one wish that would come true. It was silly, but Grandpa loved it. He insisted on getting it for me.'

'And did you make a wish?'

'No, of course not,' she said, and then she winked at me.

'You did, didn't you?' I couldn't help but smile. Since yesterday, I'd seen a whole new side to Grandma.

'I wished that we would have a lovely house with a garden… I was a bit materialistic in those days.'

'And?'

'Your grandpa got promoted shortly after and we bought this place,' she said. 'It was good timing as I found out that I was pregnant with your mum. It was huge compared to the tiny flat that we lived in before. It was a coincidence… Or maybe not?'

I didn't believe in magic, and yet there was something in Grandma's story that made me wonder. Maybe there was the wildest possibility that I too could harness the power of the key and use it to bring Jack home.

'Here, have some breakfast,' Grandma motioned towards some croissants. 'Gertrude has found a tolerable jam.'

My mind was racing with everything I wanted to tell Keira and update on the tree.

As we ate, Grandma told me more about her travels with Grandpa. I still couldn't quite imagine her backpacking in the Amazon rainforest.

'On the second shelf of the white bookcase in the living room, you'll find a row of photo albums. If you want to see more of our travels, you can have a look at the dark green one. Why don't you bring it here?'

I found it quickly and brought it back to the table. I flipped open the front cover and saw another copy of the same photo that was in the bedroom on the front page.

'Can I borrow it to have a proper look?' I asked her.

'Yes, if you promise to bring it back. I like to look over it sometimes and reminisce.'

'I promise.'

I was putting the album in my bag and preparing to leave, when I noticed a series of framed posters on the wall behind Grandma Sylvie's head. Each had a small illustration and French words written in a swirly font.

'What are those?'

'Ah, Gertrude found them at an art exhibition. They make me laugh. Jack loves that middle one the most.'

'*N'oubliez pas de vivre*,' I read aloud. A small girl wearing a red hat was smiling, staring up at a vast blue sky, where a single bird, a tiny 'V' shape, was disappearing into the sunset. She immediately made me think of Margot. There was a look of hope on her face and she filled me with a new optimism.

'What does it mean?' I'd always been terrible at French, much to Mum's disappointment.

'Don't forget to live.'

'Don't forget to live? It's not the kind of thing you'd forget.'

'It's *exactly* the kind of thing people forget,' Grandma disagreed. 'They are often so engrossed with their jobs and the tiny things that they do day to day, that they lose sight of what's really important, often until it's too late.'

She was right. Of everything my brother had been accused of, forgetting to live was not one of them.

'I need to run,' I told Grandma. 'Thank you for talking to me, and for letting me stay the night. I promise I'll ring you straight away if we hear anything.'

'Thank you for coming to visit me,' said Grandma Sylvie, 'it's been wonderful to see you.' And for the first time in what seemed like ages, she pulled me in for a bony hug.

Nine

It was freezing outside so I borrowed one of Grandma's thick cardigans for the cycle home. The rain had finally stopped, and the gentle touch of sun made everything appear brighter. I took a shortcut through the field, the sandy path sparkling and crunching like sugar under my wheels. In the tufts of grass at the edge of the playing field I spied the tiny green humps that promised daffodil leaves. I hoped that the frost wouldn't get to them before they managed to flower.

But when I got home, hope evaporated. Mum looked so pale that I wasn't sure whether she'd gone to bed at all. Last night's phone call had clearly made her feel worse about everything. I knew Pickles was only doing his job by updating us, but I couldn't help but feel annoyed with him.

The news on TV no longer featured regular updates on the earthquake, so Mum had taken to trawling the internet for any smidgen of information she could find. She was sitting on the sofa scrolling frantically on her laptop. She reminded me of a sad ghost.

'Hi, pet,' she said, looking up as I walked in. I noted the flicker of surprise at my cardigan, before she remembered where I'd been. 'How's Grandma?'

'Yes, she's fine. Gertrude is nice. Grandma really seems to like her.'

'Oh that's good,' she said. 'And how are you feeling?'

'All right.' A part of me wanted to tell her about everything that I'd discovered, because I thought it might make her feel better, but at the same time, I wanted to spend longer mulling over all this new information about Jack to make sense of it. So I gave Mum a hug instead.

'It's lovely to see you,' she said, braving a smile. 'You cheer us up, you know. If you want some breakfast, Dad's in the kitchen. I promise we'll try to cook something nice tonight. I'm going to do my best to drag myself away from all this news – it's not doing me any good.'

I walked down the hallway to find Dad sitting at the kitchen table, scribbling a shopping list on a piece of paper. A tuft of hair stood up on the top of his head. He looked young and helpless. Not like my dad at all.

'Are you all right?' I asked him.

'Oh, Flick. Yes, well – I'm trying to do something practical, so I thought I might go out and do the food shopping. It's all this waiting that's killing me,' he admitted, and then his brave face suddenly disappeared.

'What is it, Dad?'

'I keep thinking that if he was all right, surely he would have called us. He would always call, wouldn't he? Especially if he knew that we were worried.'

'Of course. But aren't the power lines still down in a lot of Peru?' I asked.

'Actually I think mostly the power's back to normal, apart from some parts of Lima which were badly affected.'

'Maybe he's somewhere far out though, where there's no signal.' I could hear the desperation in my voice.

'We need to be patient, as painful as it is. I just hope that Jack has enough medication to last him. How are you feeling about going to school? I can't believe it's already Monday.'

'I'll be fine. It's distracting at least.'

'That's true.'

'Dad, we'll be OK. We will,' I said, putting my arms around his neck. I don't know what made me say that.

'I keep thinking there must be something I haven't thought of, you know? Another person who might be able to help.'

'You've honestly done everything you can. And people know about Jack from the news. If they thought they could help, they'd let you know, wouldn't they?'

'You're right, Flick. Thank you for saying that.'

I poured myself a glass of orange juice and went upstairs to get changed. I couldn't resist checking in Jack's room. I knew instinctively that nobody had been there since I'd visited with Keira. I drew a new branch for Grandma Sylvie, to add to Sutty's and Manfy's. I added smaller branches for the photograph of her and Grandpa, the trick that Jack had played on her, and the story the market-seller had told about the key.

I took the key out of my pocket, carefully hanging it around my neck, and shut my eyes. I knew it probably wouldn't work, because the key didn't belong to me, but I still held it tightly in the palm of my hand and wished as hard as I possibly could that Jack would be found and that he'd come home safe. I knew how silly it sounded, but Grandma's wish had come true, so there was a tiny smidgen of hope that mine would too. I chose to keep the necklace on under my shirt collar for good luck.

On the way into school, Keira linked elbows with me.

'I did some more investigating of my own. I went to see Grandma Sylvie.'

'Seriously?'

I filled Keira in on last night's visit.

'Aha, so it's not her,' she said, disappointed.

'No. She's not S.F. At least not the S.F. that Jack was thinking of.'

'You've made progress, though,' she observed.

'How?'

'Well, we know from two different sources how much Jack loved playing the guitar. We also know that he enjoyed matchmaking. And most importantly, you know where the key originally came from. That could be crucial.'

'True. We've gathered lots of information, now we need to sift through it to see which bits are useful and to try to somehow fit them all together – that's the hard part. But we can do it. I know we can.' I thought of mine and Jack's detective partnership and how positive he always was about us finding a solution to every riddle.

'Hey, I was right about Finny, or should I say, Mr Shane Finnegan – another S.F. Shall we speak to him today? I found out on the school website that he teaches orchestra until 5 p.m. I can message my mum and say we're going to After School Club and get her to pick us up at 5.30 p.m. That way we can catch him before he leaves. What d'you reckon?'

'Sounds like a plan.' I didn't feel hugely hopeful about speaking to him, but Keira was so enthusiastic that I couldn't say no.

Later that morning we had English and I was relieved that we were continuing our detective crime fiction. When I was writing Lady Abigail and Margot's story, I forgot about everything else. It was as though the rest of the world didn't exist. Mrs Emmett caught my eye and gave me a reassuring smile, but she said nothing and I was grateful to her.

I was glad to dive back into my writing.

Lady Abigail sat in the corner of the dark sitting room. One of the maids scuttled in every half hour or so to ask whether she would like the fire lighted, but she told them firmly that she did not. She felt that she no longer deserved the comfort of light and warmth. She should have held Margot's hand in the crowd. She should have kept a better eye on her.

Margot had always been such a badly behaved girl, not like her friends' daughters. She would get into trouble by playing tricks on some of the other children, she'd rip her best Sunday clothes when climbing trees and would get lost in public places because some curiosity had taken her fancy. But this time was different. The disappearance wasn't Margot's fault. It was clearly the fault of her abductor, who had only left the bell symbol as a clue.

When she saw it there, pinned to the inside of the beret, Lady Abigail's first thoughts flew to Edwin and Louisa Bell – old friends of her husband's who lived off Thames Street. They'd been nearly as wealthy as the Jacksons themselves a few years ago, but had lost their fortune when Edwin's brewery went under and were now almost bankrupt.

They had been extremely kind to her when her husband died, and Lady Abigail refused to believe that they could have anything to do with her daughter going missing. But after getting the police on the case, she felt utterly useless, and she thought that the Bells were worth a visit, if only as friends to confide in. Although they were younger than her, Margot had always enjoyed playing with the Bell girls, Georgina and Stephanie.

As she pulled her coat around her and made her way slowly in the direction of Thames Street, she realised guiltily that she hadn't even visited Louisa since the family had fallen on hard times, six months ago now. How easy it was to forget people when they no longer made an appearance at your dinner parties.

When her old friend opened the door, Lady Abigail almost didn't recognise her. Louisa looked so much thinner, the colour drained from her cheeks. The house was in the process of being packed up – there were crates, trunks and bags everywhere.

'Oh Abigail, how good of you to visit. I apologise for the mess. We're moving to

Welwyn, you see. It's a country cottage and all that we can afford at the moment. What brings you here?'

When Abigail told her the news about Margot, Louisa's eyes narrowed with concern.

'Margot's gone?' she whispered. 'I don't know what we would have done without her these past few months.'

'How do you mean?'

'Bringing her old clothes for my girls to wear, helping me do the laundry and carry the groceries home when we let Mary go. She even packed some of these crates for us.'

'Margot did this?' asked Lady Abigail. 'You mean, my Margot?'

'Yes, you didn't know? Please let me know if you hear any news. I will be worried sick.'

Before she could stop herself, Lady Abigail pulled out the red beret from her handbag and pointed to the tiny drawing of a bell pinned to its inside.

'It must be a message from whoever's captured her,' she said. 'But the bobbies haven't

found any clues.' She could feel hot tears
stinging her eyes.

'The bell is on the Elliott coat of arms, is it
not?' asked Louisa. 'Though I can't see how
they would have anything to do with this.'

'Maybe they know something? Anything is
worth a try.' She jotted down the address in
the notebook she always carried around in
her purse and set off once more into the snowy
streets.

'Right. Your writing time is now up,' said Mrs
Emmett. 'You can continue at home. I've had a
quick look at our intranet and can see that one story
is a favourite – the story of the lost girl, Margot.
Felicity, do you want to carry on reading? I think a
lot of us are keen to hear what happens next.'

I shook my head. I couldn't bear standing in
front of the class. 'I'm sorry – not today, if that's
OK. Maybe next lesson?' I mumbled. 'I need to
tidy up a few bits of the story.'

'No problem,' said Mrs Emmett quickly. 'Who
would like to volunteer?'

A girl called Vera, who was new, raised her hand and we listened to her murder mystery set in the middle of the Sahara Desert.

'Come on, read your story,' said a quiet voice behind me. I didn't have to turn around to know that it belonged to Duncan. I felt his gaze again, and this time I stared right back at him. His cheeks reddened and I felt a strange satisfaction at having caught him in the act.

After lunch we had geography, and were starting a new project about building a school in a remote part of the developing world. We had to choose a country and a region, and then research its people, politics and natural resources. We were asked to think about the challenges that we might come up against when planning our new school.

I decided to choose Peru, even though I worried that the tiny drummer might raise his sticks. I typed 'Arequipa' into the search bar and zoomed in on the area of the Peruvian Andes that appeared on the map. I discovered that it was a city with beautiful white buildings made of volcanic stone and framed by three volcanoes. I imagined Jack exploring with his new friends, struggling under the weight of his rucksack. He was never good at packing light. He always thought of things that might be useful, like a big ball of rubber bands, or an old wind-up film camera, which he insisted on bringing on holiday to France.

On the national tourist board website, I found that the area was close to the picturesque Salinas National Park and had plenty of fertile land for growing crops. Education was compulsory and free up to secondary school, but apparently there were many remote regions where it was not known if children actually attended school. There were some schools being built in these areas by charity organisations, but it seemed as if there was more demand than schools being built.

I flicked through the images of Peru that came up in the online gallery, and saw photos of the Inca ruins, the Nazca lines (huge patterns in the rock made by ancient civilisations), and backpackers trekking through the rainforest. In one image of a traveller, I thought I saw Jack's grinning face and quickly moved on to another website.

'For your homework,' Mr Bemowski said, 'I'd like you to prepare the first part of your PowerPoint, which will give an overview of the country you've selected. Next week, I'll select five of you to present, and then I'll give you individual feedback through the usual online homework system, so please be sure to submit everything by 7 p.m. on Sunday.'

I found myself strangely looking forward to this project. I couldn't wait to go home and get stuck into the research. I could even use the photo album that Grandma had given me as one of my sources. I had such a connection to Peru, and yet I knew so little about it. And I needed to change that fast – because somewhere on its vast sand dunes, among the rainforest rivers and valleys of lush greenery, or maybe in one of the bustling cities with their unusual buildings and architecture, was my brother. And wherever he was, I was determined to find him.

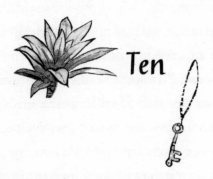

Ten

When the final bell went that day, we headed for the library to wait until the end of orchestra practice.

'Why don't we go to Sutty's to see if Simon is there?' Keira asked.

But I couldn't face seeing both him and Finny in one day, so I persuaded Keira to do some geography homework with me instead.

I could tell the entire time that her mind was drifting and as five o'clock struck she pulled me in the direction of the school hall.

'Where are we going? Aren't we supposed to be waiting outside the staffroom for Mr Finnegan?'

'What would you do without me, Flick?' she asked, winking. 'He's obviously not going to be in the staffroom. In fact, he's hardly ever there. Mostly he's in one of the music rooms or the school hall, doing band practice.'

Keira was proving to be an excellent detective herself. I was so glad to have her working with me on this.

I'd seen Mr Finnegan, a.k.a. Finny, many times before, but I'd never actually spoken to him. Finny had long, dark hair tied in a ponytail, and a wispy beard that seemed in urgent need of grooming. He was extremely tall and thin, so that whenever he sat down he looked as if he was folding himself into quarters.

He had a reputation for being adored by his students and I'd heard how he would high-five his class when they'd played a piece particularly well. We waited for ages at the back of the hall as he finished talking to members of the orchestra, giving them tips on different aspects of their performance.

It was only when he picked his bag up to leave that Keira pulled me towards him.

'Hi,' she said cheerfully. 'I'm Keira and this is Felicity, Jack Chesterford's sister.'

Finny's face immediately fell. 'I'm so sorry about what's happened,' he said gently.

I wasn't expecting such sympathy, so I awkwardly stood there, not knowing what to say. Luckily Keira came to my rescue, as she always did.

'Do you mind having a quick chat with us? Obviously Flick is missing Jack a lot, and we thought... that it would help to talk with you about his music. She doesn't have any of his recordings at home, do you, Flick?'

'Erm... no.' I wasn't sure where she was going with this, but Finny seemed to take the bait.

'Absolutely, have a seat,' he said, motioning to two vacant orchestra chairs.

I sat down where one of the violin players had been sitting, and Keira perched on a piano stool.

'Where to start? I mean, the guy really loves his guitar. Seriously, he has an ear for music. When he came to me for the first time, I was sure that he'd been playing for years. He did "Nothing Else Matters" by Metallica and I was completely speechless. Do you know it?'

We both shook our heads, but if Finny's opinion of us went down a notch, he didn't show it.

'Well, anyway, he played it and it Totally. Blew. Me. Away. And then when he said that he was mainly self-taught and had only bought his first guitar a couple of months before, I didn't believe him to begin with. I'm not normally one for complimenting people, you know. I say things as I see them. But with him, I knew that he had talent. I asked whether he wanted to be a session musician.'

'You mean like someone who tours with a band, playing guitar?' I asked. Maybe Grandma Sylvie had been wrong?

'Exactly.'

'And what did he say?' The faint drumming was starting at the base of my skull. I recalled sitting under Jack's skylight and him showing me a heavy magnifying glass that he'd found in an antique shop. I remember distinctly that he said, 'I want to be a detective. Loads of people are doctors, lawyers, bankers. But when did you last meet a real, excellent detective?' It struck me that Dad wouldn't like this career choice, but I didn't say anything at the time.

'He said that it wasn't for him,' said Finny.

'He wants to be a detective,' I surprised myself by saying it out loud. Jack's secret, released into the open, suddenly sounded ridiculous.

'Really?' Finny raised an eyebrow. 'He told me he wanted to be a teacher.'

'Like you?' asked Keira. I noticed that she'd been looking at Finny with admiration and swooping her braids behind her back every time she spoke to him.

'Well, not so much like me. I teach sixth-form music and university students in the evenings. He wanted to teach younger kids. Before he left, he signed up to do a course in Music Therapy next year.'

'Music Therapy?'

'Yeah, you know, teaching young children with various difficulties to overcome them through music.'

I was dumbstruck. I wondered if Dad had any idea that Jack didn't intend to take up his uni place to study Law, as planned. Dad had even arranged extra work experience at his chambers before Jack was due to start.

'Jack worked with a young lad called Will at Little Angels which I think inspired him.'

This part I'd heard. Jack had talked about the lunchtime reading sessions in Year Thirteen that they'd been doing with kids at the nursery down the road. He'd particularly taken to Will, who was four and was delayed with speaking. Jack would tell me over dinner how it took him several weeks to persuade Will to say his name.

'I honestly thought he couldn't speak,' Jack said, showing me a picture that Will had drawn him, which had pride of place on his noticeboard. 'But it turned out that he was just nervous. He couldn't bear to talk to anyone he didn't know, and all the lights and sounds overwhelmed him. As soon as I got him to chill out, he got much better.'

I realised now that I'd never asked Jack how he'd managed that, but I had a feeling his guitar had been involved.

'Did he sing to him?' I asked, not quite able to picture Jack keeping a straight face while singing to a room full of little terrors.

'I think he took him out of the classroom into a one-to-one room and played to him. Eventually Will was intrigued and started asking questions about his guitar. Then he opened up a bit and eventually Jack encouraged him to read aloud. Everyone was amazed, most of all Will's teacher.'

'So he definitely said that he wanted to teach?' Keira asked. She'd stopped twisting her hair and was slowly tapping her foot on the floor, which she always did when she was thinking hard about something.

'I think that was his plan, yeah.'

'And did he say what age group?'

'No, I don't think so. I'm not sure if he'd thought that far ahead. I suppose he loved working with younger kids, so my bet would be on that,' said Finny. I could see that, like me, he was confused by the way the conversation was going. He started packing away his own guitar and I sensed that he was itching to leave. My gaze fell on the tiny key-shaped hole in his guitar case and I remembered the final question I needed to ask him.

'Do you know anything about a key? One that Jack wore on a chain around his neck?'

For the first time, I saw a glimmer of recognition.

'The Inca key?'

'Sorry?'

'He told me about the Inca key when I was covering detention once – this was long before Jack started doing guitar lessons with me. He was there for playing a joke on Mr Bemowski – it was the week before Christmas. He'd set a series of tiny alarm clocks to go off at three-minute intervals throughout the lesson. They were hidden under every third desk in the room and they each played a few notes of "All I Want for Christmas Is You". Mr Bemowski found out that Jack was the culprit, because he was the only one looking at his watch and trying not to laugh. He later said that he wanted to find out how quickly somebody in his class would figure out the pattern, and also whether they'd realise what song it was.'

Keira was giggling behind her hand and Finny himself had a glimmer of amusement in his eyes as he told the story.

'Mr Bemowski didn't see the funny side?'

'No. He set Jack a piece of research into what he would recommend as the next Wonder of the World and why. Jack clearly didn't see this as a punishment. He was so absorbed that he was the last one in the form room when everyone else had left. I started talking to him about it and he told me all about this Inca gold and the key that was linked to it.'

'The Inca gold? What's that?'

'Well, I think he took the word "wonder" a bit too seriously, as in something that makes you wonder.'

'Like a riddle?'

'I suppose. He'd read somewhere about these amazing treasure chests that were stolen from a Peruvian cathedral. Apparently the jewellery in them had been mined by the ancient civilisation of the Incas and had been passed down through the generations until it was eventually hidden by a group of priests in the vault of a church. Then, one day, it mysteriously vanished. Jack said that the strangest thing about it was that the vault seemed completely untouched.

'This meant that the priests began to accuse one another, because somebody must have used the key to get the treasure. But the mystery deepened when it became apparent that the key itself was missing.'

'Seriously? Did they find it?'

'I don't know, because we'd reached the school gates by then and both had to go home. I noticed that Jack had been fiddling with something at his throat as we were walking. When I asked him what it was, he showed me the key. I should have confiscated it because you're not allowed jewellery, but I didn't. I asked him jokingly if it was the key to the Inca gold. He just laughed.'

'And you never spoke about it again?'

'We never had any reason to. In fact it was only about a year later that Jack came to me wanting to do guitar lessons. By then I'd forgotten all about it.'

'Until now,' I said quietly.

'Until now,' he agreed.

As we walked out of school with Finny, my brain was brimming with information about Jack. The tiny drummer was beating out scrambled beats – each one a tiny snippet of a melody, but none of them coming together in a recognisable song. Sometimes the beats overlapped and the noise got so loud that it caused a pain in my temple, but my feet kept walking beside Keira, moving towards her mum's waiting car.

Eleven

'He wasn't on the trip!'

Mum's yell tore me from the murky depths of a dream. I'd been standing in a dimly lit underground cavern, a glass door before me. From behind it came the gentle strumming of a guitar. As I crept closer, I made out a familiar silhouette sitting in a chair, swaying gently to the music. I banged on the door, but nothing happened. In my left hand I was holding a bunch of keys – maybe a hundred. I was struck with the awful realisation that only one of them would open the door. Then I heard Mum's shout.

I switched on the light. It was the middle of the night. I could hear Dad's frantic voice from the kitchen. I crept to the top of the stairs to listen.

'What do you mean? He was going. He said he was going! He told us he would get on the bus to Lima so that he was there when Simon arrived at the weekend, and they'd go on to the national park.'

'He didn't get on the bus. They checked all the records.'

I tiptoed downstairs and sat on the bottom step, listening.

'What does this mean?' asked Mum. Her voice sounded as if it was coming from underwater.

'I suppose it's good news for us. Quite a number of the people on that trip have now been confirmed dead, haven't they?'

Mum mumbled something in response.

'Sorry. Sorry. Obviously, I didn't mean it like that. Their poor families... But it means he's still out there. I'm certain he's still out there,' said Dad decisively.

'But where? The last time that we spoke, he distinctly said he'd signed himself up for it. If he didn't end up going, then where is he? Hold on, didn't Jack say something about this in his voicemail?'

I heard Dad scrambling around for his phone and then Jack's voice resounded so clearly that he could have been standing right there in the kitchen. It sent a jolt up my spine.

'Hey, Dad, if you get this within the next hour, call me back. If not, I'll try you again tomorrow. This week I'll be heading to Arequipa and then hoping to catch the Lima bus so that I can meet Si when his plane comes in on Saturday night. We'll go to Paracas and then later maybe to Cusco. It's a bit touristy and not the cheapest, but hey, I'm sure I can wangle myself a discount using my charm. Si's excited to join me. We've been arranging logistics already. Love to Mum and Flick. Adios.'

'It's a case of finding out where he went instead. I've already spoken to Simon and he says Jack didn't specifically talk about any change of plan although he did mention "a surprise" which we don't know anything about. We're going to have to keep thinking.'

Simon. I should have gone to see him yesterday when I had the chance. Without his address, my best bet was to ask Sutty. I didn't want to bother Mum or for her to find out about my playing detective before I had something more concrete to tell her. As I crept back to bed, I made a mental note to locate Simon as soon as possible.

'Right, what have you got for me?' Keira asked as she collected me for school the following morning. She had by now fully assumed the role of junior police inspector investigating a disappearance. Maybe she thought that by using phrases borrowed from TV, I'd forget that the investigation we were conducting was actually to do with Jack.

'He didn't go on the trip to Lima,' I told her. 'It's such good news, Keira! It means that he probably stayed further from the centre of the earthquake and that it's more likely he's safe.'

'Hey, that's amazing,' she said, giving me a big hug.

'I also did a bit more research into the Inca gold… I kept wondering what Jack would have said to Finny if they hadn't gone home that day. I looked into the different theories of what may have happened to the gold. Some say that it's been taken by pirates to a remote island off the coast of a town called Pisco, others reckon that it's buried somewhere deep in the Amazon jungle. There are even sources that claim it was shared between a group of wealthy merchants living in the capital, Lima.'

'But how did they manage to get in without a key?'

'Easy. The thief made a replica. You need a piece of clay to use as a mould and then you can make another key. The priests all knew the guard and I was reading somewhere that it's most likely that one of them managed to sneak the original gold key out when he was taking a break. It was a case of knowing him well enough to predict his behaviour.'

'Sort of like what we're doing with Jack?'

I hadn't thought about it that way. 'I suppose… Anyway, this legend is so famous in popular culture that there's now an Inca Gold Bank and an Inca Gold Monument. And there are other things dedicated to the key itself.' I wondered whether Jack would have tried to go into the jungle to find the treasure. Was that the 'surprise' that he'd mentioned?

'Lots of useful facts. Have you put all this up on the tree?'

'Yeah.' Earlier that morning I'd completed a whole branch of Jack's tree that was dedicated to Finny, and to the Inca gold.

'So the mission for today is to speak to Simon, right?'

'Exactly. Let's see if he's at Sutty's after school.'

That morning through double maths, I couldn't concentrate. Mr Rox was off sick so we had a supply teacher who'd set us a whole page of mind-numbing equations from our brick of a textbook. I was exhausted from lack of sleep and I hid behind its open pages, my head on the desk. The numbers swam before my eyes and morphed without warning into the figures that Mum had taken to studying on the screen – the growing list of the dead and injured in Peru. And that horrible gnawing question at the base of my skull, which caused the drummer to spring into action.

Where was he? Where was he? Where was he?

'Where are you?'

It was only when I felt Keira nudging me that I realised I had asked the question aloud.

There was a titter of laughter from the boys in the back row.

'Are you all right?' asked Miss Killian, the supply teacher. She was young, probably not much older than Jack, and she looked petrified. She'd probably never yet come across a student who had lost the plot.

'Yes, fine,' I muttered. The blood rushed to my cheeks.

'Do you want to get some air? Or maybe see the nurse?' she asked.

I could only manage a nod. I stood up and walked out of the classroom.

The empty corridor stretched before me and I felt a surge of relief. I sat on the steps leading to the second floor and stared vacantly into space. I had no intention of going to see Nurse Minton, who gave out paracetamol for absolutely everything, from sore throats to, in Keira's case, a broken wrist.

I thought about going to Sutty's to find Simon. I could probably sneak out for half an hour without anyone asking questions. They would think I was with the nurse, and before they realised I wasn't, I would sneak back.

I was about to go when a wall display caught my eye. It was of the sixth form trip to India the previous year. It had been organised in partnership with a charity called Rolling Earth, which built schools in parts of the developing world. I peered at the photos – there he was. Jack was standing in front of a colourful and bustling marketplace with his arms slung around a couple of friends.

In a burst of memory so powerful that he could have been standing right next to me, I saw him as he returned from the trip. I'd just recovered from a stomach bug and was lying on the sofa watching films and feeling sorry for myself. He'd been dropped off by one of his friend's parents and strolled in looking browner than ever. Mum and I gave him a big hug and bombarded him with questions, because we hadn't been able to speak to him. We knew that we wouldn't be able to contact

Jack for most of his trip, because the village where he was staying was so remote that it didn't pick up phone signal. We'd only received a quick message as he arrived at the airport, to say that they had landed safely. Remembering this made me feel slightly better about losing contact now. Maybe he couldn't get to a place which had a decent connection?

That day we sat him down on the sofa and asked everything that we'd stored up over the past ten days. Where did you stay? What were the people like? Was the food incredible? Jack answered all our questions, but I could tell there was something on his mind.

It was only later, when we were sitting under his skylight waiting for the 10.15 p.m. to New York, that he told me.

'We spent most of the trip in a "bamboo hotel" near Kochi, but we each got to spend a day with one of the local families who lived in this tiny village in Kerala. It was the most incredible experience. My family were the Lagharis. They had eleven kids and ran a small farm. They had so little but their house was always immaculate. The older kids looked after the young ones and everyone was happy. And they had this amazing school.'

'Amazing, how?'

'Get this – they saw how important it was for their kids to get a good education but at the same time, they needed as many adults as possible to work the land. So their solution was to get the old people in their community to teach. They figured these people couldn't do hard, physical work any more, but they had many years of knowledge. There were some who had even been to school outside the state. And you could tell that they loved teaching. They only taught a few lessons a week each, so they never got too exhausted. The kids really bonded with them and they would visit them either at home or at the local social club for the elderly – they became like adopted grandparents. It's a great idea, isn't it?'

'I suppose,' I said. 'It's great that they could make it work.'

'We don't do anything like that here,' said Jack, 'and it's a real shame. I feel like we forget about older people. Take Grandma, for example – there's so much about her that we don't know, because we've never bothered to ask. I feel like I'm only beginning to get to know her.'

Something told me that this memory was significant to our current search, but I wasn't sure why. I jotted it down in the small notepad which Jack had given to me, and which I always carried in my rucksack. It was something that might come in useful later.

Twelve

'**W**hat are you still doing here? Aren't you supposed to be in the operating theatre?' asked Duncan, striding out of class first as he always did. The operating theatre was our class's name for Nurse Minton's room in which nothing medical ever happened.

'Erm, yeah, I've just come back,' I lied. I couldn't believe I'd been staring at the display for almost fifteen minutes.

'Are you feeling better?'

'A little. Still not a hundred per cent.'

'Sorry to hear that,' he said, and then followed my gaze to the photo cabinet. 'Are you hoping to go on one of these trips?'

'Maybe one day. Jack went on this one,' I muttered, tapping my finger on the glass, 'that's him.'

'Oh,' he said, peering closely at the photo. 'I really hope you hear from him soon.'

'Thanks.'

'At least Mrs Emmett is trying to take your mind off things by getting you to read your Victorian story to the class.'

It took a few moments for his words to sink in.

'Are you saying that she's doing it out of pity?'

Any good opinions that I'd formed about Duncan disappeared in an instant.

'No, no that's not what I meant—'

'—You think my writing isn't any good?' I interrupted. 'That otherwise nobody would be interested in the story?'

'I'm not saying it isn't good. With some polishing up it could be great.'

'"Polishing up"? Is that a phrase that you learned on a writing course or something?'

'Well, actually, my dad runs one and he's been teaching me...'

But I didn't stick around to hear any more. Keira

appeared by my side and I grabbed her by the elbow and together we walked off in the direction of the canteen for lunch.

In geography, our final lesson of the day, we continued working on our projects and I tried hard to push Duncan's comments out of my mind. I concentrated instead on researching Rolling Earth, the charity that Jack had volunteered with in India, and which had since extended its work to Nepal, Myanmar and Vietnam.

Frustratingly, there was no mention of any schools being built in South America. We would have to cast the net wider. But how? It would be impossible to contact every school in Peru.

I was struck again by the scale of the task I had taken on. How many clues I'd been presented with, each one as useless as the next, because none of them seemed to bring me any closer to finding Jack. I needed space to think and to make sense of everything I'd found so far. Everything I'd uncovered, all the people I'd spoken to, raced through my mind and Duncan's words echoed cruelly, 'It could be great, it could be great...'

While Keira was talking to Mr Bemowski about her project, I dashed out of the classroom before the bell went for the end of the day.

Even though it was barely half-past three, the streets were already cast in the half-darkness of late January. The sky was a murky yellow, like clouded mustard – the suggestion of rain, or maybe a heavy storm. The wind had gathered pace and my ears were hurting from the cold. I pulled my hood up tight.

As I turned into the high street I spotted a smudge of red glowing against the gloomy street. My heart leapt – there she was! The girl in the red beret was walking ahead of me, swinging a spotted umbrella in her left hand. I could tell from her powerful stride and the curl of her hair that she was the same person that I'd seen from the window.

She crossed the road and I followed her as she merged with the afternoon shoppers and crowds of people milling around the bus stop. Then she stopped on a street corner where an older man in an oversized coat was collecting money for a sick children's charity. 'Margot' – because this is what I called her in my head – dropped some money into the collection bucket and spoke to him for a few moments. I was now close enough to see her smile as she shook his hand. Her smile was so powerful that he started grinning too and I felt for the first time since Jack left that everything would be OK.

I wanted so badly to run up to her and touch her hand to make sure that she was real. But I stopped myself – she would probably think I was mad.

I couldn't resist hurrying after her as she continued down the road, past the old library and the town hall. She walked so quickly that I could barely keep up, and then I saw the red beret dart to the left – she must have turned into one of the side streets.

I picked up my pace, frantically scanning the street that I was sure she'd walked down and then the next one, in case I'd got it wrong. But Margot was nowhere to be seen.

I felt the prick of tears in my eyes.

'Where did you go?' I whispered. I was slowly turning around to walk back in the direction of home, when I found myself standing by the entrance to the Fairwick Estate. It was as though Margot had led me here.

As I walked to the entrance, I had a sudden flashback to when Jack and I had first discovered the magic of the estate. We were helping Dad bring the shopping home, and we had heard shouting above our heads.

'It's just some kids playing,' said Dad dismissively, but Jack was clearly intrigued. He kept glancing back at the estate building long after we'd passed it.

'There must be a playground or something up there on the roof,' he told me, amazed. 'I could hear them playing football.'

We checked it out after school the very next day. The Fairwick Estate was six floors high, with an arch instead of a front door, which was lucky for us as we could go in without anyone asking questions.

The alleyway that led to the building from the main road was dark, winding and uninviting. But Jack convinced me that there was more to the place than what you saw at first glance. Although the walls were greying concrete, they somehow held different hues of orange and yellow when the sunshine hit them at the right angle. The corridors and stairwells could definitely use a lick of paint, but walking along them we got the distinct sense that they would lead somewhere special – and they did.

When I opened the door to the rooftop my legs ached from walking up six flights, but I was so relieved to be there. The air was different on the roof – lighter somehow and fresher. Jack told me that it was further from the pollution caused by the buses, taxis and other cars on the high street.

I imagined the pollution particles, small, spiky urchins. If I strained my eyes enough I could almost see them; each detaching from its cluster, emerging slowly from an exhaust pipe or office window and floating up into the charcoal sky.

I was pleased to see that nothing had changed. My mind felt clear for the first time in ages. I perched in my usual spot on the old roundabout. It had been some architect's grand design – a playground on a rooftop. There was fencing all around and a sturdy sheltered area for rainy days. But what this big thinker was not aware of was that Fairwickers were not the sort to be told what to do. Give them a playground and they'd turn it into a football pitch or an open-air recording studio.

I loved the roof of the estate. I'd decided that I loved it the very first time that Jack had brought me here. There were possibilities on the roof that existed nowhere else. Possibilities for brain space and clearer thoughts, or more precisely *a* thought, that ran in circles through my head.

I took out my phone and looked at the photo I'd taken of Jack's tree. It had five branches now – Sutty, Manfy, Grandma, Finny and Sol, although this last branch needed to be replaced with Simon.

'What are the facts, Flick?' I heard Jack's voice in my ear.

'These are the facts, Jack,' I said aloud into the cold winter air.

'One: You've been missing for five days.

Two: You're somewhere in Peru.

Three: You didn't go on the trip to Lima, which is a really good thing.

Four: You love playing guitar.

Five: You like teaching. It's something I didn't know.

Six: You can't speak Spanish, or at least not very well, so if you wanted to do voluntary teaching, you would probably teach English. (This had just occurred to me. It meant that the pool of schools to call would be smaller than I had originally thought.)

Seven: You are very kind, kinder than most people know.

Eight: You have a key that used to belong to Grandma, which was given to her by Grandpa when they were in Peru, long before Mum was born, but you left it behind.

Nine: I have found five people with the initials S.F. which you left with the key, but none of them seem to think it was meant for them.'

'Although we haven't spoken to one of them yet...' said a voice behind me, 'and maybe we should because he could have something interesting to say.'

Keira sat down next to me and gave me a tight hug. I squeezed her back.

'I miss him,' I whispered, 'I really miss him.'

'I know,' she said. 'You've been incredibly brave. Try not to cry. You won't be able to think properly if you cry. And your brain needs to be working to solve Jack's riddle.'

I put my hands to my face and noticed that they were wet. I hadn't even realised that I'd been crying.

'How did you know I would be here?'

'I remembered you telling me how much you and Jack used to love this place.'

'Yeah, he really enjoyed coming here and looking at the view. Look, you can see our house and he knew every building on the horizon.'

'Mmm... I know.'

'Keira, I'm scared it's not Simon either,' I blurted out. Had that been my real reason for coming here? A way to avoid going to find Simon?

'What do you mean? That he's not who the key is meant for?'

I nodded.

'Well even if that's true, he's not the last S.F. in the world, is he?'

'He's the last one we know.'

'At the moment, yes. But we'll keep searching

until we find the right one. You can't avoid one of our top leads though, because you're scared he might not be as useful as you think. Imagine what Jack would say.'

She was right of course. I forced myself up.

'Are we going to Sutty's?' I asked her.

'No. Simon wasn't there when I dropped in on the way here. Sutty says that he's taken the rest of the week off. I messaged Manfy to ask if she knew where he lived. She sent me his address. It's less than a ten-minute walk. If we hurry, we should be able to speak to him and still get home before six.'

Thirteen

The closer we got, the more convinced I became that it wasn't a good idea. I wasn't sure that Simon would want to see us.

'It's this one,' said Keira, motioning towards a house with a neat front garden, complete with a mini palm tree struggling against the wind, and a swing seat.

I rapped on the door before I could change my mind and a split second later it swung open. A tall greying man stood before me in jogging bottoms and a zip-up hoodie. There was a black sports bag slung over his shoulder. He was rushing out and clearly hadn't expected anyone to knock. He was probably Sol – the first S.F. whose name I'd discovered. I'd never met Simon's dad before.

'Hello, is Simon in?'

'Oh, hi,' he said absentmindedly and motioned for us to come inside. 'He's in his bedroom,' he said sighing and there was a fleeting look of worry on his face. 'Shout up to him, he'll come down,' he advised and then headed out. Before I could say anything else, he was gone. The front door slammed behind him and moments later we heard the bleep of his car door unlocking and the engine starting.

'What do we do?' I asked Keira.

'Call his name.'

'I can't. Won't he think we're right weirdos, standing here inside his house? We need to go back out and ring the doorbell again.'

She nodded and I lifted my hand to undo the lock, careful to be as quiet as possible.

That was when we heard the Spanish voice upstairs and Jack's name among the scramble of words.

I froze. There was movement on the landing. Simon was coming down the stairs, an exasperated look on his face.

He was so engrossed in his conversation that it took him a while to notice us, but when he did, he smiled a sad smile and finished the call.

'We're sorry. We didn't mean to turn up like this,' I began, 'your dad let us in…'

'It's fine – don't worry. Are you all right?'

'Kind of. Not really. You?'

'Same.'

'This is Keira,' I said. 'Have you met before?'

'Yes, at your house once. Hi, Keira. D'you both want something to eat? I've put on a pizza.'

'Sure, I'd love some,' I said, feeling suddenly ravenous. 'I didn't know you spoke Spanish.'

'Yeah, I'm not brilliant. But we lived in Barcelona when I was younger and although I went to an international school, we had some lessons in Spanish. We moved around a lot because my dad's a diplomat.'

'Oh yeah. That's why you only came to our school in sixth form, right?' I could tell that we were both avoiding the subject of Jack.

'Yeah, it wasn't easy to be honest. I'd moved schools a lot but I'd never found it that bad. It was only here that it was tough,' he said, manoeuvring the pizza onto the chopping board.

'Really? Why?'

'There were a couple of guys in our class who had it in for me from the beginning. They laughed at my weird accent and braces. It was like they were looking for someone to bully.'

I glanced at Simon's immaculately straight, white teeth and wondered whether they would be laughing now.

'It was awful. One day they cornered me after school. It was this time last year and it was absolutely freezing. They nicked my coat and emptied a bucket of water over me. By the time I got home, I was properly shaking. I got ill after that and I think they freaked out that I'd tell one of the teachers. Tuck in,' he said, motioning to the pizza and offering us both plates.

'And did you? You should have done!' I said, feeling furious on his behalf.

'No, I didn't in the end. Jack convinced me not to. He said it would make it worse. Anyway, they seemed to back off a bit when Jack, Darren and Leon made friends with me. It happened when things got so bad I was seriously contemplating quitting school.'

'Quitting? But where would you go?'

'Oh, I have no idea. I suppose I was thinking I might miss the end of the year and then start again in another sixth form in September. At the time I'd come back from school and lie on my bed for hours and hours. Dad persuaded me to go to the tennis club with him and that's where I made friends with Jack. I knew him from school, but not very well. He started inviting me to stuff with him and his friends, and slowly life became more bearable.'

'Because you had people to hang out with?' I knew that Jack and Simon had met at the club, but I had no idea about the other things he'd mentioned.

'Yeah, I think they respected Jack in a weird way and weren't sure how to react when we started hanging out. They laid off me after that. Jack was awesome. He's one of the most genuine people I've ever met.

'And now this... It was meant to be the trip of a lifetime. I'm sorry, that's a stupid thing to say,' he said, running his hand over his face, embarrassed. 'I was supposed to meet Jack there on Saturday – I'd had my stuff packed for ages. I still can't believe it.'

'I know,' I said. 'We overheard you talking to someone on the phone. Was that about Jack?'

'Yeah. I called Ariane, who Jack mentioned in one of his last emails – she's the woman who ran the trip to Arequipa, which he was on before all this happened. I wanted to find out if she knew him or if he mentioned his plans for what to do next.'

'How did you find her? What did she say?' Keira asked.

'I looked her up online and found her contact details. It's amazing I managed to get through as a lot of the phone lines are down. She was so helpful – she said that she remembered Jack very well as he'd made friends with loads of people. He apparently met an Aussie guy called Rowan there, who he hung out with for most of the trip. This guy was a teacher and he'd been volunteering at a Peruvian school. If only he'd said more in that last message...'

'What last message?'

'Jack sent me a message a few days before the earthquake, saying that he had a surprise for me. He was going to send me all the details in an email about where to meet him, which never happened. Your dad rang me the other day to ask about this, and I wish I had something more to tell him. But it looks like Jack never got a chance to send that email.'

'I have a feeling he went to volunteer at a school,' I said. I told Simon all the information we had from Finny. 'But how would we ever find out which one? I bet there are thousands in Peru. Maybe slightly fewer if you remove the ones who don't accept English-speaking teachers.'

'A school? Normally you have to sign up for these volunteering schemes months in advance.'

'But you know what Jack's like. He would have found some way around that. Or maybe this Rowan guy he met knew of a place that needed volunteers.'

Simon's eyebrows shot up as I was talking. 'Let me show you something,' he said, and gestured for us to follow him. He took us upstairs to his bedroom – a tiny room mostly filled up by his bunk bed and a desk beneath it. He fiddled with something on his laptop and a map appeared on the opposite wall to us. I noticed that Simon had done the same thing as Jack – he'd covered the wall with whiteboard paper. That way he could label the map with a red marker at specific points. There were also black dotted circles going outwards from a central location.

'This is where Jack got off the bus on Wednesday night,' he said, grabbing a pencil and tapping the centre of the smallest circle. 'According to Ariane, they arrived after six p.m. The earthquake hit before four in the morning the next day, around ten hours later. So the question is, what could Jack have done in that time? There are loads of possible answers, but the one thing we know for certain is that he didn't go to Lima, which is excellent news because that would have been really close to the epicentre of the earthquake.'

Keira tracked the circles with her finger.

'What are these?'

'The first is a rough outline of where you might get to if you walked for a couple of hours. Jack loves walking, but even he probably wouldn't manage more than a two-hour stretch with a backpack. Plus, he would have wanted to get a hostel for the night, and by the time he got off the bus, it wouldn't have been long until it got dark.'

'And this one?'

'That's a rough estimate of how far you could get by bus in ten hours. I think it's doubtful that he would have got on another bus straight away. I imagine he would have waited until morning and got one the next day, but there's a chance that he did. I wanted to leave it there as a possibility. The other thing is that he knew I was flying into Lima airport – here – and I don't think he would have made me do a long bus journey to meet him straight after my flight, so that is another thing to think about. You see this blue line, here? That's where you can get to within a five-hour bus ride from Lima. I know five hours is a shot in the dark, but I needed to have some sort of estimate of where he might have asked me to meet him.'

There was a small area like a lop-sided eye where the blue circle overlapped with the outer black one.

'So do you reckon this is where we should be looking?' I asked.

'It's a good place to start.'

There were two towns within the 'eye', Nazca and Ica. Other than that, there was a tiny lake and two large national parks, one shaped like a baseball bat.

'It's mostly desert in these parts, apart from a few areas of greenery. There are sand dunes everywhere and tourists go dune-boarding – it's the Peruvian equivalent of snowboarding. I was going to check it out with Jack, but there's quite high wind at this time of year. We'd have had sand blasted in our faces.'

'Is there a way that you could find out where all of the schools are in this area?'

Simon frowned.

'I'll see if there's anything on this map that allows me to do that.' I watched over his shoulder as he fiddled with the different dropdown menus. At first, petrol stations appeared on the map, then hospitals, and finally, he managed to locate schools.

There weren't nearly as many of them in the 'eye' as I'd imagined. They were mostly clustered in and around the towns, which wasn't surprising.

'Can you bring up the names?' I asked, not quite sure what I was hoping to see.

'I'll have to hover over them and then the name will come up. Or, wait – this programme lets me download all of them into a spreadsheet.'

Within a few seconds, we were looking at a list of schools, with their addresses and phone numbers.

'I think we need to try calling them to find out whether they have seen Jack,' I decided.

'Do you think it's possible he would have arrived at one of these schools within ten hours? Even if he'd hitched a ride, or taken a bus, he would've got there at nighttime, wouldn't he? And then the... then the earthquake would have happened,' said Keira, looking at the floor.

'Yes, but these areas were luckily outside the immediate danger zone,' said Simon. 'I checked all of this yesterday. Anyone living east of here,' he said, pointing to a dotted straight yellow line that I hadn't registered, 'would have experienced tremors and power outage. There will have been damage to buildings and some fallen trees, but no casualties reported yet.' He sounded as though he'd memorised the line by heart.

'Are you sure about that?'

'Yep, pretty sure. I've seen it on several news websites.'

I felt the tiny drummer in my head slow his frantic beat, as if reaching a calmer part of the song.

'How many of the phone lines do you think are down?' asked Keira.

'I'm sure that some of them still are, particularly in remote areas, but I managed to get through to Ariane, didn't I? Plus, I can see if there are any mobile phone numbers. Sometimes when landlines have cut out, mobile phones still work. I'll get started on the list tonight,' he promised. 'They're five hours behind us, so if it's six p.m. now, it's only lunchtime there.'

'Is it six already? We've got to run.' I pulled out my phone and saw four missed calls from home. I sent a message to Mum straight away, feeling guilty. It was bad enough that they were worrying about Jack.

Simon put his phone number into both mine and Keira's phones and assured us that he'd be in touch as soon as he had any news.

As we walked back through the dark streets in the direction of home, I felt lighter. The cold breeze brushed my face and I thought of Jack. I imagined him standing on top of a huge dune, the sand blowing against his cheeks, a powerful wind playing havoc with his hair.

Keira squeezed my hand and readjusted my hood for me. We walked together in silence and I saw her twisting one of her front braids round and round her finger. I knew that she was thinking hard about what to do next.

'We never asked him about the key,' she exclaimed. 'But maybe right now it doesn't matter.'

Fourteen

'Flick, is that you? Oh, thank goodness!' Mum and Dad ran into the hallway the second my key turned in the lock.

'I was petrified, love,' Mum whispered, 'I'm so glad you're OK.'

'I'm sorry. I'm really sorry.'

'Why didn't you call us?' asked Dad. I couldn't tell whether he was angry or upset.

'I went somewhere with Keira and I didn't realise the time. I didn't mean to.'

'It's all right – you gave us a scare, that's all. Come into the kitchen. Dinner's ready,' Mum said, making a face at Dad which meant that she wanted him to let it go.

He ignored her. 'We were so worried, Flick. You *can't* forget to call us. Not now – we have too much on our minds. We love you and need to know you're safe while we focus on getting Jack home. *Think* before you do something like that again.'

'I said I'm sorry!' I didn't stick around to listen to the rest of what he had to say. Instead, I flung my rucksack high onto my shoulder and marched up the stairs.

'Come back, Flick!' was the last thing I heard before I slammed the door to Jack's room.

I sat on the bed and stared at Jack's tree. Four of its branches were now full. The first one which had initially belonged to 'Sol Falcon' was still empty. I crossed out his first name and replaced it with 'Simon', in bold letters, as I could already sense that he would play an important role. I added in everything that we'd found out. 'Is Jack within the "eye"?' I wrote at the end of the leaf furthest to the left. I made a note to ask Simon for a printed copy of the map with all of the schools marked.

I went down to my room to get changed into

my pyjamas. I sat in bed, staring at my phone. I'd brought up the map of Peru and zoomed in to see if I remembered the rough contours of Simon's circles. The area looked even bigger than I'd first thought. It would take Simon ages to call so many different schools.

There was a gentle knock on the door. Mum peered in.

'Flick, darling, can I join you?'

I nodded and noticing that she might not see me in the half-dark, added, 'Sure'.

'I've brought you some dinner.'

She sat next to me on the bed with a plate of delicious-smelling beef stew.

'I'm OK. I ate earlier. But you should have some. It looks good.'

We sat in silence as she ate.

'I'm sorry about Dad's reaction,' she said eventually. 'You know he didn't mean it. He's... we're a bit overwhelmed by the whole situation.'

'Yeah. I am too,' I admitted, and I was shocked to hear myself ask, 'Do you think Jack's alive?' The words escaped without warning.

She opened her mouth, and then closed it again, as if scared of what she might say.

'I don't know, darling. Sometimes in the middle of the night I lie there when I can't sleep and it's almost as though I can hear him snoring in his room. But when I do manage to drift off, I have the same nightmare that haunts me over and over.'

'What happens?'

'I'm walking through the jungle with Jack holding my hand. He's about three or four – this seems to be a long time before you were born. The sun is breaking through the treetops and we're singing to ourselves. I point out little monkeys and birds, and he's giggling. Then, everything goes dark and we hear this almighty roar. It's louder than anything I've ever heard before, and suddenly his small hand escapes my grasp and... just like that, he's gone.'

'That sounds scary.'

'Yeah. And you? What do you think?' she asked carefully, and for a moment it felt as though she was the daughter and I was the mum.

I avoided answering and shrugged my shoulders. 'Have you been up to his room recently?' I was almost certain she hadn't, but I wanted to double-check. I finally felt ready to tell her and Dad about what I'd been doing.

'No. I couldn't quite face it. Why?'

'There's something up there that might interest you.'

She took me by the hand, motioning that we should go upstairs together.

Outside Jack's room, she breathed in deeply, shut her eyes and opened the door. She gasped.

'I'm sorry that I didn't tell you about this before,' I said. 'It's Jack's tree. Keira and I have been trying to figure out where he could be. This is everything that we've managed to find out so far. Each branch represents a different person we spoke to who gave us a new clue. To begin with, we mostly discovered things we never knew, or that *I* never knew about Jack – but maybe you did? Like how he helped people without expecting anything in return. Or how much he loved music, especially guitar, or how he wanted to be a teacher, and how much he cared about Grandma. Do you know that she has a new boyfriend because of Jack? He's called Mr Percy and she looks happier than I've ever seen her. I think we saw one side of Jack – the side that was easy to see. We all knew the Jack who played practical jokes on people and got into trouble. We refused to see anything else.'

Mum stared at the wall, amazed. She knelt down and touched the polaroid of Jack's face.

'You went to speak to all these people about him?' she asked. 'But who are they? I mean, apart from Grandma? How did you find them?'

I told her everything, starting from when I found the flamingo box with the key and the initials and ending with the map that we'd looked at with Simon a few hours before. I talked and talked and talked, carefully training my gaze on the tree. I couldn't bear to see Mum's reaction.

When I finished, Mum and Dad were sitting on Jack's bed, looking at me.

'I walked in as you began the story about Sutty and the ghost,' Dad said quietly. 'I didn't want to disturb you.'

The tiny drummer in my head stood poised with his sticks.

'Come and sit here,' Mum said, patting the space between them, and they both hugged me tight.

'You've found out an incredible amount,' Dad said. 'And for what it's worth, I think that you're right about him going to a school.'

'You do?'

'Yes. Most of the things that you've mentioned I didn't know,' he said, and I could hear the sadness in his voice. 'But Jack always talked about how much he loved teaching that little boy to read. Do you remember when he was researching different methods to try and build up his confidence?'

'We thought it was a school project, didn't we? But he was doing it because he loved it. I told him at the time that he'd make a really good teacher,' Mum said.

'And I stopped you straight away, and said that law offers so many more benefits than teaching. I made it sound like teaching wasn't a worthwhile career. I put so much pressure on Jack that he hid his true ambitions from me, and now I'm being hard on you too, Flick. I'm sorry about what I said earlier.'

I held him close. 'You're a wonderful dad. It's not your fault that Jack's missing. And you love being a barrister – you thought that Jack might love it too.'

'Where is this key then?' Mum asked.

I took off the chain from around my neck and showed it to her. It seemed smaller somehow than the last time I'd seen it.

'This is what it came in and the note is still there,' I said, showing her the flamingo box.

Mum opened it carefully. She brought the tiny piece of paper up close to her eyes and spent a strangely long time inspecting it. She had a funny look on her face and the corner of her lip twitched. 'You did a lot of good detective work, but maybe you didn't see what was right in front of you…?'

And it was only then that it hit me who S.F. was.

'Sergeant Flick,' I whispered.

Next to me Dad smiled.

'Obviously. Who else would it be?'

Fifteen

I couldn't get to sleep for hours that night. Two very different feelings whizzed round and round my head like loud, circling helicopters. One of them was anger. I was furious with myself for being so careless with the only clue that Jack had left me. What kind of a detective sergeant was I, if I had forgotten my own childhood nickname? But the other feeling was happiness. I couldn't remember when I'd last felt this happy and relieved. Over the past week, I'd felt I'd lost Jack entirely, as if I didn't know anything about him any more. Yet it turned out that he'd left me his most prized possession.

I eventually drifted into a restless sleep. A huge pile of keys appeared before me, of different shapes, colours and sizes. Some seemed old and were covered in layers of rust, others were brand new and glistening, as if they'd just been cut. There were thousands, maybe even hundreds of thousands of keys in the pile and the more I stared at them, the more they multiplied before my eyes. I was desperately running my hands through them, trying to find Jack's tiny key, but it was hopeless. It would take me months, maybe even years, to sort through all the keys, and even then I might never find it.

I sank to my knees and was about to give in when the pile before me began to shake. It shook and shook, the tremors becoming so bad that keys were thrown in all directions, hitting me on my head and chest and legs.

'Stop!' I screamed. I covered my face with my hands.

As quickly as it had started, the shaking stopped and I heard a familiar voice.

I opened my eyes to see Jack emerging from the pile, like a diver resurfacing from deep waters.

'Come on, Sergeant Flick,' he said laughing. 'How did you not realise that the key was meant for you? You're the only one I trust to solve our mystery.'

I was woken up early by my phone beeping. It was a message from Simon.

No luck with the schools. Managed to get through to three of them – rest unreachable. Power lines are still down in remote areas and there's been more damage to buildings. Aftershocks caused badly constructed buildings to topple, and people are trapped underneath the rubble. I'll keep trying. Wanted to update you.

My stomach clenched.

'OK, thanks anyway,' I wrote back, 'I'll let you know if we hear anything from the police.'

I was skimming through the pages of Grandma's album when I spotted a photo of her at a market stall. At first I thought she was buying earrings, but when I inspected it more closely, I saw that she was looking at lots of tiny keys. I imagined Grandpa must have taken the picture before he'd bought the very key that Jack had left behind. Below the photo, was a note that said, 'Souvenir shopping at L…' The last word was so smudged that I couldn't work out what it said. I decided that I would call Grandma and ask.

'Hello, Felicity, darling. Any news about Jack?'

'Nothing, Grandma, I'm sorry.'

'Ah, well.' I could hear her struggling to sound cheerful. 'Soon, hopefully.'

'Yes. Grandma? You know the place that you and Grandpa got engaged? Where he bought you the key? I found a photo of it in your album. Do you remember what it was called?'

'How could I forget? It was a little village called Llave, with a double L. It means "key" in Spanish. It was in the middle of nowhere and it took us an age to get there. I even got fed up and wanted to turn back, but Grandpa insisted because he'd heard from some locals about how interesting it was.'

My heart sped up.

'Did Jack ever ask you about it?'

'He did. He was fascinated by it.'

'Thank you, Grandma. I've got to run.'

I raced upstairs to get my tablet and searched for 'Llave, Peru'. I prayed that the village still existed.

A few hits came up, and I clicked on the first entry which was an encyclopaedia article.

It looked like the place hadn't changed much since Grandma and Grandpa had visited. It was pretty tiny, but there was a larger settlement close by, which was big enough to be a town. It was called Cortegana. I discovered that there were two schools.

I grabbed my phone and called Simon. He answered straight away.

'There's a village called Llave that I need you to look up, next to a small town called Cortegana. It's outside the area that you mapped, but I honestly think that Jack could be there. Could you try the two schools?'

I loved that Simon didn't ask me anything about how I'd come across these places or why I thought they were important.

'Sure, I'll try them now. I'll ring you back,' he promised.

To distract myself from the agony of waiting, I researched the history of the village. It had been founded by Spanish conquerors in the seventeenth century and for many years had been home to cattlemen and their families. Until, in the late 1920s, a local businessman opened a key factory there, which soon began supplying keys to the surrounding area and, later in the 1960s, became a tourist attraction. It was around this time that the village changed its name to Llave from its much less interesting name of Aqa.

Next, I looked up Cortegana. I scanned the article. There didn't seem anything particularly unusual about the town. It was the childhood home of a famous Peruvian film star, and was known as the remotest town in Peru, reachable only by one road. It was encircled by mountain ranges, and in all the images, I could see snow-covered peaks and dense forest.

I prayed that wherever Jack was, he was safe and had access to his medicine. I was about to close the page when something made me click on the image of the town's cathedral. This brought up a whole new entry. I scanned the page and my eyes rested on the subtitle, 'Legend of the Inca Gold'.

It was the cathedral that Jack had told Finny

about. I punched the air. Just then my phone vibrated on the desk.

'No connection at either school,' said Simon. 'But I rang the community centre in Llave and a guy called Carlos picked up. It was a different type of number so I reckon it could be a mobile. Anyway, he said that there were lots of people staying at the centre and at the supermarket next door, as they were the two larger buildings that had managed to survive the tremors. Many of the houses have been flattened. He didn't know the names of everyone staying there, but he did say that there were tourists and travellers. Loads of them were asleep, obviously – I'm an idiot for not remembering the time difference – but he took my number and he promised to send me a message if he had any news on Jack.'

'That's amazing. Thank you so, so much.'

I could tell that Simon seemed surprised by how happy I was.

'Hey, no problem. But this doesn't necessarily get us any closer to finding him, you know that, right? I spoke to a random guy who had mobile signal in a small village somewhere in central Peru.'

'Trust me on this,' I told him boldly.

It made perfect sense – this was the place where his favourite key had come from, *and* it was close to the origin of the Inca gold. I was so certain of being right that I sat cross-legged with my phone in front of me, waiting for the call. I stared and stared at the screen.

Eventually, I couldn't bear it any longer and I shoved it out of sight under the bed. My fingers brushed against something leathery – the book of riddle tales. I'd forgotten all about it. I brushed off the layer of dust from the cover and flicked through to the last tale I'd written.

The Riddle of the Locked Chest. The memory of the final riddle Jack had told me made my eyes blur. I flicked back through the notebook. There were so many stories there, easily more than a hundred. Jack hadn't known that I'd written them all down. I wondered if I'd ever have the chance to tell him. I began to hungrily read through them, wishing that I could reverse time to when I'd jotted down the very first riddle.

I was so engrossed that I didn't notice the time until a car horn brought me back to reality and

I panicked when I saw that it had already gone 8.30 a.m. Drat, I was supposed to be at Keira's, ready to walk in together. I weighed up my options. I could go into school and keep my phone in my pocket (which was breaking the rules). That way, when I heard it buzzing, I could make up an excuse and run out into the corridor to take the call.

The alternative was telling Mum that I didn't feel well and staying at home, but I knew that if I did that, I would likely spend many more hours sitting here on the bed, staring at the phone, which would be torture. Who knew how long it would take the community centre man to find Jack? I took down Jack's calendar from the wall, and struck through all the days that I'd left unmarked since the earthquake. I heard the echo of his words, 'Every day you tick off means I'll be a day closer to home.' Then I threw on my school uniform, carefully placed the key under my shirt and went next door.

The weather had cooled overnight, and instead of the glorious, spring-like morning that I'd hoped for, it left a miserable, boggy greyness and a fine, cold drizzle. The rainwater ran down the pavement causing tiny, sad-looking rivers that splashed up my leg, leaving annoying damp spots on my tights.

I ignored it, trying to keep hold of the nervous excitement that was filling me to the brim.

'Why are you so...?' Keira began when she saw me.

'Oh, Keira, I've solved the investigation. You'll never believe who S.F. is!'

'No way! Who?'

'It's me! It stands for Sergeant Flick – the nickname that Jack gave me.' And then I told her all about showing Mum and Dad the tree.

'I can't believe we did all that work and it turned out to be you! How mad is that? But you know, I don't think it went to waste. There's lots of important—'

'—He's going to call today,' I interrupted her. 'I know that Jack's going to call. He's in a village called Llave. It's where Grandpa bought the key for Grandma and it's also close to the cathedral where the Inca gold was stolen. All the clues have come together. I'm certain that's where he is.'

'Woah, slow down. How do you know all this? Have you worked out what happened when he got off the bus?'

'I think he decided a few days earlier that he would go to Llave instead of travelling back to Lima. He must have been curious about the place where the treasure legend comes from, and maybe this teacher, who he met on the bus, told him about a school in the area that runs a volunteering scheme – Simon is still looking into that part.'

'And you think Jack will be able to call from this man's phone?' Keira asked, when I'd finished updating her.

'Yeah, there's a time difference. We need to wait another couple of hours. It's still early morning there,' I said confidently.

Keira squeezed my hand.

'What's that for?' I asked.

'Nothing.' She seemed surprised, almost as though she hadn't realised she'd done it.

'You're worried I've got it wrong, aren't you?' I asked.

'No I... You know I want Jack to be found, Flick.

I've been helping you with this from the beginning. And I think we're definitely getting closer. You could be onto something, but then again, we might have to cast the net wider. I want you to understand that if you're wrong this time, it's not the end...'

I felt so angry about the tiny seed of doubt she'd planted in my head that I refused to speak again until we reached school. Because of me, we were seven minutes late and had to go into the school office to sign in.

As luck would have it, Duncan was there registering his own lateness. He gave me a nervous smile and loitered, waiting for us to leave the office. He seemed to have a sixth sense for catching me at the very worst moments.

'Hey, I spoke to my dad about your story,' he said. 'He's willing to take a look at it. He might have some useful feedback.'

Before I could answer, we heard a deep American voice ahead of us in the corridor.

'Oi, squirt, where's my hoodie?'

Duncan's face instantly changed, as if somebody had chucked a bucket of ice-cold water over him.

His features rearranged themselves into a look of worry, maybe even fear. He shifted out of my line of sight, and I could see that the person talking to him was a tall, muscular guy of about Jack's age, wearing tracksuit bottoms and a T-shirt with two crossed tennis rackets. He loomed over Duncan, who seemed tiny in comparison.

'I… I don't have it,' Duncan stammered.

'Yeah, you do,' said the older boy furiously, who I was now certain was his older brother. 'I saw you take it from my room this morning when you thought I was asleep. If you don't give it back by lunchtime, things are gonna get serious. D'you understand? They'll get even more serious than they did before. And don't think Dad is going to protect you this time!'

His eyes narrowed as he said this, but Duncan had already turned on his heel and started walking away, before I could witness more of his shame.

'Loser…' hissed Duncan's brother. 'Get Mom to buy you your own stuff! And stop pretending to be me! You're a poor imitation.'

Duncan's shoulders twitched at these words and

I actually felt sorry for him. But when he glanced in our direction to work out how much we'd heard, our faces must have betrayed us. The colour rose in his cheeks as he pushed past us.

'He's an idiot,' I heard him mutter. 'He thinks he's so great.'

'You could say that about Duncan,' I sniggered to Keira as we walked to class. But I began to understand where all of his snooty behaviour came from and felt a tiny bit guilty about being so snappy with him. He desperately wanted to be as good as his brother and his dad, I could see that now, and yet he hadn't found something that he really excelled at.

I'd noticed how awkward Duncan was in our sports lessons. He probably figured that he couldn't follow in his brother's footsteps and become a tennis star. Instead, he'd put all of his energy into writing, but maybe it was more difficult for him than he'd thought. Trying to live up to expectations made people behave in different ways – Jack avoided our dad, while Duncan clearly did everything to get the attention of his.

The first two lessons of the day were maths and I couldn't concentrate at all. I kept sneaking my phone out of my pocket to double-check that I hadn't missed any calls. Jack's face, which I'd changed to my screensaver, stared back at me, unblinking.

'But,' I kept telling myself, 'it's only 5 a.m. there...' Then 'only 6 a.m.' and 'only 7 a.m.'. As the hours mercilessly ticked away, I felt less and less sure of myself.

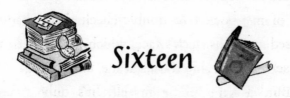

Sixteen

After break we had English again. Mrs Emmett pulled me aside at the beginning of the lesson and asked whether I would read my latest extract to the class. 'Only if you want to, Flick.'

I'd already refused once, so I nodded reluctantly. It was the worst possible timing. What if I got the phone call right in the middle of reading?

'We only have two more lessons in which to finish off our crime thrillers,' Mrs Emmett said, banging the palm of her hand on the desk to signal quiet, 'so hopefully you should be getting to the heart of your story by now. I'll make sure that I leave ten minutes at the end of the lesson to hear some of your creations. Meanwhile, you have forty minutes to get on with your writing. I also have an important announcement to make, so don't let me forget.'

I managed to collect my thoughts enough to focus on the story. It was a welcome relief from constantly worrying about Jack.

When Mrs Emmett called me to the front, I slid my phone to Keira under the desk and made her promise that she'd signal to me if it rang.

Behind us, Duncan scrambled around with his books and pencil case, accidentally dropping things onto the floor which he then had to noisily pick up. I wondered if he was deliberately trying to sabotage my reading. Any regret I'd felt at snapping at him vanished in an instant.

'Duncan, when you've sorted yourself out, perhaps you would like to volunteer?' said Mrs Emmett coldly.

'Maybe later,' he mumbled. 'I'm not really ready.'

'I've called this story "The Case of the Beret and the Bell",' I told everyone. 'This is the part after Abigail has found out from her old friends what Margot has been doing to help them.' As I started reading, I felt strangely self-conscious, as if I was revealing a secret part of myself to the class.

'Who is Margot?' The question swirled around and around in Lady Abigail's mind as she went about her day. It had replaced her previous question, 'Where is Margot?' because it seemed more important.

The bobbies had been no use – they were too busy catching pickpockets and vagrants to worry about a young lady going missing. Lady Abigail felt so desperate that she had decided to begin her own investigation. But the more she found out, the more she realised she didn't know her daughter at all.

Over the past week, since visiting Louisa, she had uncovered many surprising things about Margot and written them all down as a list at the back of her pocketbook:

- *Helping the Bells when they were struggling*
- *Visiting and caring for an elderly neighbour who was very sick*

- *Helping the maids with the Christmas preparations so that they could leave early to see their own families*
- *Handing out money to the poor begging outside St Paul's Cathedral*
- *Secretly giving reading lessons to Sally, one of the cook's daughters, who wanted to go to school but had to work alongside her mother.*

To Lady Abigail it seemed that wherever she turned, somebody knew Margot and remembered something wonderful that she had done. She felt terrible that she hadn't known any of these things about her own daughter. She would still have tried to stop Margot from doing them though. After all, helping the maids with their work was not a task becoming for a young lady.

And yet, despite Margot's goodness, somebody had set out to snatch her from her family. The thought of her daughter lying in a cold, dark cellar somewhere and in this freezing weather, made Lady Abigail feel sick. Recent stories in The Illustrated London News *told of a child-snatcher who had been nicknamed 'The Bearded Fiend'. It was believed that he had stolen eight children so far and was using them to start a ring of thieves in the west of the city.*

The Bearded Fiend seemed to operate in the Chelsea area, which was far from the Jacksons' home, but she feared that he could have extended his reach.

Lady Abigail found that she could no longer eat. She couldn't sleep. She suffered from waking nightmares so severe that they left her in a cold sweat.

One day when Henry was having his eggs in the dining room, it occurred to her that her son, although quiet, hadn't seemed anywhere near as distraught by Margot's disappearance as she was. She decided to ask him why. Henry was startled by the question.

'Because I don't think that she has been snatched, Mother,' he admitted eventually.

'What do you mean?'

'You believe that Margot's been taken, but maybe... Well, maybe she chose to leave.'

'You're saying she disappeared on purpose?' asked Lady Abigail. She couldn't accept the words even as she said them.

Henry nodded.

The red beret, which the bobbies had returned after deciding it offered no further clues, was hanging on the carved wooden coatrack. Lady Abigail wouldn't admit it to anyone, but she took it to bed with her every night.

Henry glanced at it now as he finished his breakfast.

'They sell them outside the hospital, Mother. They are worn by the nurses. They raise money to look after the poor and infirm; those destined for the workhouse.'

'What? Henry, why did you not mention this earlier?'

'I didn't think it mattered.'

'Which hospital is it? St Bartholemew's?'

'No, the Evelina Hospital. The children's
hospital near London Bridge.'
Lady Abigail put on her coat, drank a glass
of water which the maid passed to her, and
headed straight for the door.

This was as much as I'd managed to write and I
felt it was a good line on which to end the chapter.
I glanced back at the class. I'd almost forgotten that
they were there. I looked over to Keira hopefully,
but she shook her head. He hadn't called.

'Thank you very much, Felicity. Very intriguing.'

Next, we heard from Duncan's sidekick, Max,
whose story was surprisingly good, and from a
shy boy called Errol who'd slightly misinterpreted
what we were supposed to be doing and had written
a complicated sci-fi crime comic, complete with
detailed illustrations.

Finally, Duncan strolled up with his next
instalment of 'The Cabin'. By now, I was certain
that everyone in the class must have figured out that
the weapon of death had been an icicle.

'Thank you, all,' said Mrs Emmett at the end

of the lesson. 'Before you go, I want to announce something exciting. There's a countrywide new Young Writers' Award which has been brought to my attention, and a particular part of it is dedicated to crime fiction. It's one entry per school and I'd like us to take part. Having read your stories, I've selected five which I think are particularly strong, and I want you as a class to help me choose the one we should submit. We're mature writers in this class, so it isn't a popularity contest. I trust you to be fair and not just to vote for your friends.

'The people whose stories I've shortlisted are: Vera, Max, Felicity, Siobhan and Rafe.'

An excited murmur went round the room. Normally, I would have been thrilled at the news, but I felt nothing. I couldn't even muster a smile when Keira slapped me on the shoulder.

Behind me, Duncan was boasting about all the big literary prizes that his dad had won.

'I'm pleased for you, dude,' he said eventually to Max, and then more quietly, 'we'll make sure you win, yeah?'

Seventeen

By lunchtime, Jack still hadn't called and I couldn't wait any longer. I sneaked away to a far corner of the netball courts and rang Simon. He picked up on the first ring.

'Nothing,' he said. 'We need to keep waiting. I'll try calling again in a few hours, but I don't want him to get annoyed with me. I'm sure there are loads of people trying to find their friends and loved ones.'

'You know you don't have to stay here,' said Keira when I updated her, 'you can go home. Everyone will understand.'

But for some reason, I insisted on staying in the lunchroom, staring at my plate, picking at my chips. I thought going home might jinx things – that Jack definitely wouldn't call if I gave up on my day.

I was trying to avoid everyone's gaze, even Keira's. I could see Duncan throwing me odd looks from behind one of the canteen pillars.

'What does he want now?' I muttered to Keira.

'Oh, ignore him. He's an idiot.'

But as we were putting away our trays, he walked over to us nervously, clutching something in his hand which, on closer inspection, seemed to be a folded piece of paper. I could tell by the way he was holding it that he didn't want anyone else to see it.

Before I could ask what he was playing at, he thrust the clammy square into my hand and was gone.

Keira was burning with curiosity.

'I'm not in the mood,' I told her, putting the paper in my jacket pocket. 'It's probably information about one of his dad's creative writing courses or something. I'm not going to give him the satisfaction.'

My phone was silent through the last period of double chemistry, and when Keira's mum came to collect us, I told her that I would rather walk home on my own. Her eyes widened in surprise and worry, but she agreed.

'Message your mum and tell her that's what you're doing,' she made me promise.

I took the long route home, dragging out each step. Remembering what Charlie had said, I took my phone from my pocket and messaged Mum.

Back late, I wrote simply. *Don't worry x.*

I walked past the edge of Ottoman's Field and sat down at the corner, exhausted. The last few days had been cold, but I hadn't noticed quite how freezing it had become. It was only when I stopped moving that I regretted not wearing my proper winter coat. As I was pulling my thin jacket tightly around my shoulders, it began to snow.

At the other end of the field, a group of kids who'd been playing football stopped their game and looked up at the sky with wonder.

As the snow continued to fall, I squinted. Through the flurry of white, I could make out two figures spinning round and round. One was small and chubby with pigtails, wearing a thick woolly hairband, and the other was tall and skinny with long arms that flew outwards as he turned.

'Look, it's settling on the ground, Sergeant Flick,'

Jack shouted, 'we can make snow angels.' And he picked me up and threw me in the air, before we both toppled down and lay there, flapping our arms to make angel wings.

I stared and stared at those two angels, willing them, more than anything, to be real. My eyes stung with the cold and before I knew it, streams of tears were running down my cheeks and my shoulders were shaking.

'Are you OK?'

I hadn't noticed that one of the kids had run over to me – a young girl, her hair swept up in a messy ponytail, her cheeks red from the cold.

'Oh yeah, fine,' I muttered.

I forced myself to stand up and walked slowly in the direction of the high street. My feet took an unexpected left turn, and I found myself outside Uncle Michael's old flat. He'd lived there on his own for many years before he'd met Auntie Hannah and set up Gilmore's, and he'd sometimes offered to look after us when Mum and Dad went out, although Jack always insisted that he didn't need babysitting. I loved being at his place, mainly because, like me, he was a big fan of reading, and gave me books that he'd enjoyed as a kid.

From the outside, the flat looked exactly the same as it had done when we were small. Even the balcony that we'd spent so much time on was still covered in ivy. Jack had loved that he could be completely hidden, while spying on everyone who passed below in the street.

I had a memory of an old man standing on the pavement, smoking, and Jack singing in a low voice: 'You're having such a lovely puff, but your lungs are shouting "Please, enough! We're filled to the brim with awful tar and soon we'll end up in a jar!"'

The man had frantically turned around to see where the song was coming from, and not seeing anyone, quickly stamped out his cigarette and made a run for it.

I'd dangled my feet through the rails of the balcony and laughed so hard that my stomach hurt.

I wished that I could be up on that balcony now, looking down at the world below, but new tenants had been living there for years.

As I stood gazing at the balcony, the snow began to settle more thickly, and that beautiful blanket of white made even the drab, grey buildings seem somehow magical. I stopped for a moment and watched the fairy-dust flakes falling into the open palms of my hands. Then, out of the corner of my eye, I saw a smudge of red. Margot! She passed me on the other side of the street, wearing her red beret. My first instinct was to call after her, but something stopped me. Instead, I followed her, my boots filling the footprints created by hers.

She sang as she walked. I couldn't hear the words, but it was a beautiful, upbeat melody. For a moment, I shut my eyes to savour the soft snowflakes on my face, and the sound of her song. When I opened them again, she was gone. I looked desperately around for the red beret, but it was nowhere to be seen. Instead, I found the dilapidated entrance to Fairwick Estate a few feet away from me, seeming to invite me inside. I realised how much I wanted to be up on the roof.

But when I got closer, I could hear voices from above. I groaned inwardly. Some local kids must have rediscovered the playground and were playing in the snow up there. I thought of turning back. I wasn't used to sharing the roof with anyone other than Jack. But something – perhaps the smallest possibility that Margot could be up there – led me to climb the stairs.

The murmur of voices grew louder the higher I went. I cautiously opened the door.

'Flick! You made it!'

And there they all were – Sutty, Manfy, Simon, Keira, even Finny.

'All of Jack's tree branches,' Keira whispered in my ear. 'I was planning to bring you here after school and then you escaped! But it looks like I know you too well – you seem to have wandered in this direction anyway,' she said, smiling.

'But... but what are you doing here?'

'We're here to show you that you're not on your own,' Keira explained, hugging me tight. 'I hoped to bring your grandma, too, but the lift is still out of use and we'd struggle to get her wheelchair up the stairs. She sends her love and I said that we would try to FaceTime her later.'

'But how did you manage to get everyone together?' I asked, amazed.

'I messaged Simon and Manfy at morning break. Then it turned out that Simon knew Finny too – I mean, Mr Finnegan,' she said, glancing over at him and blushing, 'so he emailed to find out whether he might be free. And then I went to Sutty's shop on the way here, and he was closing up, so… we all made it.'

We sat down in my favourite spot, behind the roundabout where you could get the loveliest view of our town. Keira had brought blankets, mugs and a thermos of tea. She'd even thought to bring her spare coat and scarf, which she handed to me.

Finny took his guitar from its holder and started strumming a familiar tune. It was an interesting piece, which had long, slow and steady parts, giving way to an exciting, upbeat melody.

'I love that,' I told him. 'What is it?'

'It's called "Octopus's Garden" by The Beatles. It's a song that your brother always loved playing. In fact, I think it's one of the first full pieces of music that he learned off by heart.'

Manfy, who was sitting cross-legged next to me, pulled something out of her bag and gave it to me.

'I know it's not perfect,' she told me, 'but I think I did a pretty good job.'

I looked down to see a beautiful black and white photo of Jack. His head was tilted back and he was laughing at something. In the background I could see the shelves of Sutty's shop.

'Thank you,' I said, hugging it to my chest.

'And an evening of Jack would not be the same without his favourite snack,' said Sutty, taking a huge box of chocolate frogs from his rucksack.

'It doesn't matter if your theory is wrong, you know,' said Simon. 'You've done so much. Look at this.' He'd brought a print-out of the spreadsheet which listed all the schools he'd contacted. There were almost fifty on there.

'It was you who called them,' I corrected him.

'Yes, but only because you asked me to. And you would have done it yourself if you could speak Spanish. I bet you've done more than the police have to find Jack. It's incredible.'

I felt warmth rising in my face despite the freezing weather.

'Promise us you won't give up hope,' said Manfy. 'We won't if you won't.'

I looked around at all of their faces staring at me anxiously, and I said, 'I promise. Of course I do.'

Then we sat eating chocolate frogs and drinking tea from Keira's thermos. Finny continued to play and the snowflakes swirled around us. The tiny drummer in my head had not made a reappearance the entire time that I'd been there, and I had stopped frantically checking my phone.

'I said that we'd call your grandma,' said Keira, passing me her phone, where Grandma Sylvie's face appeared on the screen.

'Hello, darling,' she said. 'I wanted you to know how proud I am of you. I probably didn't tell you enough when you were small, but there it is. I think your brother would be amazed at how far you've come with your search.'

'Who is it, Sylvie?' I heard a man's voice in the background.

'It's my granddaughter, Martin. Do you want to see her?'

And then a large face filled the screen.

'You can't go that close,' Grandma said, 'pull it away a bit so she can see you.'

'Ah yes, hello there. I'm Martin. Your grandmother always talks about you. Maybe we can meet in reality one day?'

'I hope so,' I told him.

'Hello, Mr Percy,' said Manfy, looking at the screen over my shoulder.

'Samantha! Lovely to see you again. What are you doing there?'

'I'm with Flick. We've had a gathering of Jack's biggest fans.'

'Ah, that's fantastic. Everyone at St Austin's misses him, me especially. I hope so very much that you hear from him soon. Stay warm!'

The sky was almost entirely dark now and the light from our phones wasn't enough to see by.

As we started to head home, I asked Manfy, 'How do you know my grandma's boyfriend?'

'Mr Percy? He does the gardening at St Austin's

nursing home. I used to go there with Jack every Thursday afternoon after he'd finished his exams. We would play guitar to the residents. It was nothing like I imagined. The men and women who live there have such interesting lives. We could listen to them talking for hours. And they seemed to love us playing to them. Sometimes they would put in requests for songs that they hadn't heard in years. Jack would play them the octopus song – the one that Finny was playing. One old man even brought out sheet music for a piece that he composed back in the sixties. He really wanted us to play it. We practised for a few weeks to try and get it exactly right...'

But I was no longer listening to what Manfy was saying, because an idea had formed in my mind which I needed to act on straight away.

Eighteen

Nursing homes. Why hadn't I thought of it earlier? It all made sense. Jack serenading Grandma and getting her together with Mr Percy, his love of the Rolling Earth schools employing older teachers, and now, the visits to St Austin's that Manfy described.

His words came back to me: 'I sometimes feel like we forget about older people.' But maybe in Peru they did things differently? Maybe there was some sort of organisation for the elderly that he'd found and wanted to visit? It was a long shot, but it was definitely worth a try.

'Sorry,' I said to Manfy, 'I've got to dash. Simon, would it be all right if I came to yours on the way home? Just for ten minutes?'

'Yeah, of course,' he said, surprised. 'What is it?'

'Let's look up old people's homes near Llave,' I said, as soon as we got through his front door.

I was glad to see that his parents were out. I felt I couldn't waste time explaining anything.

We ran up to his room and Simon switched on his laptop. But the search in Spanish brought up no results.

'Nothing at all?'

'Nothing in the immediate area. Remember that it's a remote town. I reckon that most families in rural Peru are able to take care of the elderly themselves. They probably don't use nursing homes as much as we do. Hold on, let me try the search in English, just in case,' he said, seeing my disappointed face.

We saw the top search result at the same time.

Oro Homes – free accommodation in return for your time.

Simon clicked on the link.

Why not stay in one of our breathtaking treetop hostel rooms nestled among the Chila mountains, in return for your voluntary work?

Oro is a retirement community with a difference. Apart from our core team of regular staff, we rely on voluntary support provided by tourism. Our residents come from all over the world to enjoy our wonderful setting in the Chila mountain range.

We encourage volunteers from a host of different countries to stay with us and spend time with the men and women who have made Oro their home. Voluntary work can include reading, playing games, listening to music and sharing life experiences.

In return we offer beautiful treetop accommodation with unforgettable views. Stays can range from two weeks to three months.

The more I read, the more my heart sped up.

'Call them,' I said to Simon, before I noticed that he'd already picked up his phone.

'No connection. They're pretty far outside the town, look,' he said, enlarging the online map of the local area. 'And they could be quite high up in the mountains. If there are a lot of fallen trees their access to the roads might be blocked. I imagine the phone signal is usually patchy, let alone now.'

'Shall we contact your guy at the community centre to see if he knows anything?'

Simon checked his watch and called the number.

For ages nobody picked up. Then I heard a sudden *'Buenas tardes'* on the other end of the line.

Simon started speaking in Spanish and I waited, frantically picking at the skin around my fingernails, like Mum when she was stressed.

Then, the man's voice went quiet, although Simon still held the phone to his ear.

'What's going on?'

'Wait,' he mouthed at me.

Then the voice returned and Simon's eyebrows shot up.

'Gracias,' he said, *'muchas gracias.'*

'There's a backpacker at the centre from Oro,' he told me, as soon as he'd disconnected. I noticed that he was trying hard to keep his voice steady. 'He came into town last night. He says that he remembers a British guy who turned up just as he was leaving Oro. He matches Jack's description. They've had charity food aid delivered by helicopter at the community centre – the trucks would have taken too long to get there because the place is so far out. Apparently the same charity had been to the nursing home and made a delivery there. It sounds like the people are OK. They have no electricity, their access is blocked off and the phone lines are still down, like I guessed, but they're otherwise fine.'

'Oh my goodness. What do we do now?' I asked Simon. I could feel my arms shaking.

'I think your parents need to tell the Foreign and Commonwealth Office. They'll know who to contact on the ground in Peru.'

'But we still don't know for certain that it's him,' I said, struggling to contain my excitement.

'No, we don't, that's true,' said Simon carefully. 'But his physical description matches almost exactly.'

I ran home as fast as I possibly could. When Mum opened the door, I could barely breathe.

'There's been a sighting of somebody who looks a lot like Jack,' I told her, 'I think I know where he is.'

I told my parents what Simon and I had managed to find out and within minutes, Dad was on the phone to the FCO. He had me on speakerphone so that I could add in any information that he'd missed. The woman on the other end said that they would let us know as soon as they had news.

'But Flick, how in the world did you find this out?' Dad asked, amazed, after he'd put down the phone.

'Just by piecing together the clues, one by one – like Jack taught me. It was through Grandma and Jack's friend Manfy that I found out about him playing guitar at St Austin's and I took a gamble that he might want to do something similar in Peru. As for why we searched in that part of the country – well, that's a longer story.'

'I still think you should tell us about it. I'd like to hear.'

The three of us gathered in Jack's room and I talked Mum and Dad through my latest research.

'I can't believe he went to play to the elderly residents,' said Dad. 'And Grandma knew about this? Why didn't she tell us?'

'Maybe she thought we knew?'

'Why didn't Jack tell us?' Mum asked.

'That's the main question,' Dad agreed. 'It's because he thought we had a certain opinion of him, and he'd given up trying to make us change it. But he has, without knowing it, in the biggest way possible.'

It must have been around three in the morning when we finally fell asleep – me and Mum in Jack's bed and Dad on the floor.

The sunshine was already streaming in through the window when we were woken up by the phone ringing downstairs.

I leaped up and ran down to the kitchen.

'Hello, can I speak to Mr Chesterford?' the voice asked.

'Have you found Jack?' My voice came out in a croak.

Dad gently took the receiver from me, introduced himself and repeated my question. He put the man on speakerphone.

'Yes, we believe we have. We can't be one hundred per cent certain, but one of the Peruvian rescue teams has located a young man who matches your son's description in the Oro resort. We've transported him to the nearest hospital in Cusco. He's being treated for some minor injuries, but we should be able to speak to him later today. If we ascertain that it *is* Jack, we will of course get him to contact you right away.'

'He has haemophilia. The doctors need to know that he has it. His blood doesn't clot properly, so it's very important that he has regular injections.'

'Ah OK, I do believe that the doctors may already be aware of this. I will confirm though.'

My heart raced against my chest. If they were aware, then it had to be him.

'Who is it?' I heard Mum's frantic voice behind me.

'They think they've found Jack.'

There it was. I'd said the words that I was scared I would never say.

I still couldn't believe they were true when I sent them in a message to Keira, to Simon and to Manfy, and later when I repeated them to Grandma on the phone.

But I needed to hear Jack's voice to make sure that it was real.

'Please can I be the first to speak to him if he calls?' I begged Mum. After all, I'd been the one to find him. It was only fair.

Mum and Dad let me take the day off school especially. The phone rang after lunch. Every part of me believed that the call would come, but I was shocked when it happened.

It was a beautiful, cold day at the end of January. The warm sun shone for the first time in days. Outside the window, the determined heads of daffodils were already beginning to emerge – specks of brilliant yellow among the sea of green.

I'd been sitting in the kitchen with Mum and Dad eating blueberry pancakes, which we'd all made together, like we used to on the weekends.

My hands shook as I held the receiver but I managed to keep my voice steady.

'Hello?'

'Flick? Is it you?'

'Yes, it's me,' I said, as if it were the most normal thing in the world.

'You won't believe how happy I am to hear your voice.'

'Same,' I said. And then the tears came. I couldn't hold them back any longer and they flooded down my cheeks like rainwater.

'It turns out that you managed to solve the biggest mystery of your career to date without my help.'

'I suppose I did. Are you all right?'

'Yes. It's been horrible, but I was lucky. I always am, aren't I?'

His voice was exactly the same and it sounded as though he was smiling. I imagined him now with his mouth turned up at the corner.

'You are, always,' I told him. 'Will you come back now, Jack?' I asked, suddenly freaked out that he planned to carry on travelling.

'Obviously, Sergeant Flick. You can't continue to do all your work alone. Even the best detective needs a sidekick, so I'll be back to help you. I promise.'

Nineteen

On Saturday we were all at the airport, waiting for Jack's plane to land – me, Mum, Dad, Simon and Grandma Sylvie, in her new wheelchair and wearing her best red lipstick. Mum clutched my hand. I think neither of us would believe that Jack was truly safe until he was home with us. What if something had happened to him on the way to the airport? What if he didn't make the flight?

I hadn't told anyone, but that morning I'd woken from a nightmare. Jack was about to get on the plane when a giant hand appeared out of the sky, slowly forming a fist which pounded the runway and made the ground crack. I woke up shaking.

But when we arrived at the airport, things seemed more reassuring. A few minutes earlier we'd heard an announcement that said the flight from Lima had landed with no delays, and yet my back tensed even tighter. I stepped closer to the arrivals gate as a group of people began to emerge. The hall was suddenly full of children's excited shouts and the steady, rhythmic rolling of suitcase wheels. The sun beamed, reflecting the black tiles beneath my feet. I shaded my eyes with my hand, breathed deeply and waited.

Around me, people hugged friends and relatives who had just landed, and the steady trickle of newly arrived travellers seemed to dwindle. My throat tightened. And then, through the sunshine, I saw a person walking towards me – a head of blond hair, a pair of angular shoulders, a fast, familiar walk.

'Sergeant Flick.'

He was suddenly there, with his arms around me, as if nothing had happened, as if he'd been here all along. And then Mum and Dad joined us, to complete the family hug which we'd missed for so long. I breathed in Jack's familiar smell and all the fear and distance was gone.

We all wanted to keep touching Jack when he got home, as if to make sure that we hadn't imagined him – that he was *really* there. And when we'd eaten and he was sitting on the sofa, we finally heard the answers to all the questions from when he was missing.

'I found out about Oro from a man I met on the bus,' he told us.

'The teacher called Rowan?' I asked and Jack looked impressed.

'Yes, exactly. He'd been there the previous month and he told me that the whole project was quite new, so they hadn't recruited many volunteers. He said he'd learned so much in his short time there and met some incredible people who he was still in touch with. I asked where the place was, and he showed me on the map – that was when I saw that it was close to the village of Llave.'

'It's as if it was meant to be,' said Grandma Sylvie, smiling. 'It's where I went with Grandpa all those years ago.' I looked at the framed photo of the two of them that I'd copied from Grandma's album and placed with the other family snaps on the mantelpiece.

'I know, and I'd wanted to visit that area at some point in the trip because it's near Cortegana, where—'

'—The legend of the Inca gold originates,' I said.

'Exactly,' said Jack and raised his hand to high-five me. 'How amazing a coincidence is that? Anyway, we called the Oro staff from his phone, and they actually had a couple of spaces available that week, so I thought it would be a great thing to do with you, Si, before we moved on anywhere else.

'I was already pretty close to Oro, so it made sense. They had another volunteer arriving from the UK the same day as you were meant to fly in, so I thought you could get a transfer together. It's tricky to find it – it's nestled among the mountains and you can only get there using one narrow road.'

'So you went straight there?' Mum asked.

'Yeah. It was such an easy journey, considering. I arrived late in the evening and I was shattered so I checked in and went straight to bed. I was given one of the treetop rooms and I couldn't wait to see the view in the morning. Everything was so clean. They even asked if I needed sterile water for my injections. I tried to message you, Mum, but there was no signal in my room and I didn't have the code for the WiFi, but I figured I would go to reception the following morning and get it sorted out.

'As you know, that never happened. A few hours later I was woken up by the room shaking. My bed was literally sliding across the floor.

'I ran outside and managed to get down the ladder. There was an older man who had been sitting in a wicker chair in the lobby area and his chair had toppled over – he later told me he'd gone down there because he couldn't sleep. I helped him to his feet and he kept telling me that it was going to be all right.'

'It must have been terrifying,' Mum said.

'Yeah. The shaking stopped and then started up again, harder this time. There were tree branches falling around us and one of the treetop rooms came crashing to the ground. People were screaming and the manager was shouting instructions, but I couldn't understand everything because they were in Spanish. I started panicking – I thought the shakes would keep getting bigger and bigger. But luckily they didn't – all of a sudden they eased off. It was the weirdest thing – as though somebody had switched off the engine of the earth.

'We were incredibly lucky, because we only got the edges of the earthquake. Even the buildings were mostly fine, other than some smashed windows and roof tiles falling off. It turned out that nobody had been staying in the treetop room that collapsed, which was a relief.'

'The poor residents though. It must have been awful for them,' Mum said. She was sitting next to Jack and had grasped his knee as he'd been telling his story.

'They were surprisingly calm, although some of them had had some pretty serious falls. Then we had to evacuate the building before the management confirmed it was structurally sound, and later the big clean-up job started. I helped check that the residents were all OK and get them medical help.

'The internet was down and there was no phone signal. The only landline they had wasn't working. I kept trying to think of ways to get through to you, but I couldn't. The only road into town was blocked with fallen trees. It's around a twenty-minute drive into Cortagena and I thought about walking to try and find a phone, but my help was really needed. There were so many elderly residents who were either injured, or in a state of shock. The ones with dementia were particularly badly affected. The staff were doing all they could, but they needed as much support as possible before proper help arrived. You must have been mad with worry – I'm so sorry.'

'It's not your fault, Jack,' said Dad and he pulled him close. 'We're so incredibly relieved that you're safe and that you're back. I know that there are some families who haven't been nearly as lucky as us.'

I'd never seen Dad hug Jack like that before and later that night, after I'd gone to bed, I heard the two of them up in Jack's bedroom talking about uni. I shouldn't have, but I sat on the landing and listened. I was hoping that Dad would tell Jack what he'd said to me and Mum, and he did.

'I've been really unfair,' I heard him say. 'You need to do whatever makes *you* happy. Not me or anyone else. That's the single most important thing.'

Twenty

The Young Writers' Awards Ceremony was held after the Easter break in a big hotel in central London.

The winner from our school had been announced a couple of days after Jack came back, and I'd completely missed it as I hadn't been checking online.

'Well done,' said Duncan's sidekick, Max, as soon as I came into our form room the next morning. 'You totally deserve it. Yours was clearly the best of our stories. I voted for it.' Then several other people came to congratulate me and it all sank in.

'I can't believe I'm going to the awards,' I told Keira. 'What do I need to do? Who do I bring?'

All my questions were answered by Mrs Emmett. I was allowed up to six guests, so I invited

Jack, Mum, Dad and Keira. And then I asked Mrs Emmett and Grandma Sylvie if they would come too. I could tell that Mum and Jack were chuffed that I'd invited Grandma and that she'd agreed to come.

The main hall of the hotel was already filled with people when we arrived and I felt lightheaded.

'Goodness, it's like the Oscars,' Grandma whispered excitedly. 'I never thought in my old age I'd get to see somewhere so grand again.'

'Can I see your ticket?' asked a lady in an immaculate blue uniform.

I put my hand in my coat pocket and was surprised to find two folded pieces of paper. One was the ticket, which I handed over, and the other was a small, grubby-looking square that looked as if it was torn from a notepad. As we sat down, I unfolded it and found a note in perfect handwriting.

I'm sorry. I'm an idiot. Your writing is incredible, and well... so are you. D.

P.S. I have a small present for you – a red beret. It made me think of you and Margot.

'What is it?' Keira whispered, peering at the piece of paper in my hand. 'No way, is that from Duncan?'

'Is he serious?' I asked her, and I felt the heat rising in my face.

'Obviously he is. I've always told you.'

I was still thinking about the note, when a man appeared on the stage, and the chatter subsided.

'Welcome to the first national Young Writers' Awards,' he said. 'Thank you for joining me and a very warm welcome to you. I wanted to begin by congratulating those of you who have been nominated by your schools to enter. You've already come an extremely long way to get to this stage.

'As you know we have four different categories that we'll be awarding prizes for – sci-fi, travel, romance and crime fiction, with first, second and third prizes for each. In between each category, we'll hear readings from three famous children's authors, who I'm sure you'll all know and love.'

It was just my luck for crime to be the last category. But over the next hour I found that I was enjoying myself as I listened to the different authors reading their stories, and I almost forgot about being nervous.

When the third and second prizes in the crime categories were announced, I felt gutted that I hadn't had a mention. There was no way that I would ever win it, but I had secretly hoped that I might have scraped third, or even second, place.

'And the winner of this category is really not your usual crime fiction. It's an entry that got the judges thinking because it's a study of our personalities, a story about the importance of allowing others to be themselves and to do what they love. It's entitled "The Case of the Beret and the Bell" and it's by Felicity Chesterford. I strongly urge you to read it if you haven't already.'

'It's you,' said Jack ecstatically, nudging me in the ribs. He'd been home for over a month, and I still couldn't get used to him being next to me. My fingers instinctively searched for the key around my neck, where it would now stay for ever. 'You deserve it, Sergeant,' Jack had said, giving me the key the night he arrived home, 'in recognition of your outstanding work.'

'And the first prize in this category is a family weekend away in a cottage in Torquay where the famous crime writer Agatha Christie wrote some of her stories. Is there anything you want to say, Felicity? What was it that inspired "The Case of the Beret and the Bell"?'

I froze. Why hadn't I paid attention to what the previous winners had said? All I knew is that they seemed to have had a long list of people they wanted to thank. Many had notes which they whipped out especially. Unlike me, they must have thought that they had a good chance of winning.

But then Keira wolf-whistled and the sound somehow spurred me into action.

'Thank you,' I said, and I was surprised to find that I sounded much calmer than I felt. 'I honestly didn't expect to be at this event and I really, *really* didn't expect to be up here on stage. It's true that "The Case of the Beret and the Bell" isn't a typical crime story, although it started out as one. My brother inspired me to change it into something a bit different. So now it's more of a mystery about people… Because it turns out that even the people you think you know well can be a very cryptic puzzle. There are layers and sides to a person that you can't uncover until you have the right clues. To solve somebody's personal mystery takes a lot of work but you can discover brilliant things if you manage to crack it. Anyway, I hope you enjoy Lady Abigail's search.'

And then the audience applauded, and I saw Mum and Dad looking chuffed, and Jack cheering with his arms raised high. As I walked down the steps towards them, my hands were no longer shaking. I put them in my pockets and felt the outline of Duncan's note. I heard the echo of my own words in my head – 'Even the people you know well can be a cryptic puzzle.'

I remembered that he had clapped along with everyone else when I'd been declared our class's nominee for the Young Writers' Awards and he looked like he genuinely wanted to congratulate me. He had even given me a hopeful look when I'd recently bumped into him in the locker room. At the time I'd thought he was being weird. I decided that I might invite him to the rooftop playground

soon and have a proper conversation for the first
time ever.

That night, we sat down on Jack's bed under the
skylight. He was still in his suit, and I was in the
posh navy dress that I'd borrowed from Keira.

'Were you scared up there on stage?' he asked me.

'Only for a moment. Once I got over the shock of
how many people were in the audience, it was OK.'

'You were amazing. And you're a great detective,
you know. A great writer, too. You never told
me that you were into creative writing. Or is this
something that you discovered more recently?'

'No, I've loved it for ages. You know all the
riddles that you told me? I wrote them down to use
as ideas for stories in the future. I'm still planning to
develop them into a story collection when I get the
chance to write them. I'm not sure why I didn't tell
you. I suppose I wanted to write something that I
was really proud of first. Otherwise they would be
empty words...'

Jack sat up properly then and looked at me.

'What you've just said – it's how I've felt for as long as I can remember. I wanted to do something that I was proud of, you know – something impressive, that I could tell you and Mum and Dad, my plan for the rest of my life, or at least for the next few years.'

'And do you know now?'

'Well,' he said, reaching up and opening the skylight. 'I'm closer than I ever was. And as soon as I'm certain, you'll be the first to know, I promise. I'm glad that we get to hang around for a bit longer before I go to uni. I know you're thinking that it'll be different after I go, and it will, but I'll always come back. I don't think I'd last too long in the field without my sergeant.'

He squeezed my hand and I knew that he was right. Things would be different, but maybe I was ready for that. If the search for Jack had proved anything, it was that I, Sergeant Flick, was stronger than I thought.

'Are you glad you went to Oro, despite everything?' I asked Jack.

'Absolutely – I don't regret it at all. It's the most awesome place. I hope we might go together one day.'

'*N'oubliez pas de vivre?*'

He laughed. 'You saw it at Grandma's? I'm glad you went to visit her. Not forgetting to live is especially important if there is something that might be stopping you…' he said quietly.

'Like your blood?'

'Yeah, for example. But everyone's different.'

And then he turned to me and said, 'Hey, will you read me the ending of your story? I still haven't heard it.'

'Sure.'

Lady Abigail had never set foot in the Evelina Children's Hospital before. Her family had always been treated by the private surgeon, Dr Marshall, so she hadn't had reason to visit one of these ghastly places. With the recent epidemics of scarlet fever and TB, the hospitals were packed, and there were rumours that you were more likely to contract one of these illnesses by visiting an infirmary than by doing anything else in the outside world.

The market stall that Henry had mentioned was by the hospital entrance and was run by two young, dirty-looking street boys. Lady Abigail was shocked to see that they were both wearing the exact same beret that Margot had. On the small table was a display of knitwear, all in a bold, blood red that made her eyes hurt. She picked up one of the berets and noticed the pin straight away. The little paper cards with bells were attached to everything.

'How can I help you, ma'am?' asked one of the lads. He was surprisingly confident for a street urchin.

'Why do they all have this tag? What does it mean?' she asked.

'The picture? It's the symbol of the Bell Foundation, ma'am – the charity that supports the little nippers.'

Of course. How wrong she had been about the whole thing.

'My daughter's missing,' Lady Abigail heard

herself say. 'She owned one of these. She must have bought it here.'

'What does she look like?' asked the smaller boy.

As Lady Abigail described her daughter – her flame-coloured hair, freckles and unusually long legs – she could see their eyes light up.

'You mean the lass who works at the hospital? The young nurse?'

'Sorry? No. No. That's not the one. She doesn't work anywhere. She's only thirteen,' said Lady Abigail, and then coughed awkwardly, realising the boy she was speaking to was probably no older than ten.

'Well, there's a lass called Margot who we know. She must look like your daughter,' said the boy shrugging.

'Margot? That's her name! Where is she?'

'She's with the nurses in the infant infirmary,' he replied, indicating a door to her left.

Lady Abigail ran into the building that had always repulsed her so much. The stench hit her as soon as she entered – but she ignored it.

She called to the nearest nurse, a burly matron in a huge apron and white cap.

'Sister, is there anyone called Margot here?' she asked. 'I'm looking for my daughter. Do you know where she is?' Tears were spilling from her eyes now and she couldn't stop them, no matter how embarrassed she felt.

The nurse looked Lady Abigail up and down. 'Our Margot?' she asked. But seeing her desperation, she eventually nodded and said, 'Come with me, madam.' They walked together down the long corridor, where the cries of infants could be heard from behind the doors on either side. It sounded as though there were hundreds of them, all in pain, all needing someone's love. It brought to mind the Christmas collections at church to support orphanages – Lady Abigail made a mental note to donate more money. She would donate her entire fortune just to know that Margot was safe.

'She's in here,' said the matron. 'This is the ward where we treat abandoned babes. A sorry *number of them are found on our doorstep at this time of year, and some of them suffering from scarlet fever. There are a lot of families out there who cannot feed another mouth and they count on our help.'*

'Can I guess what happens next?' asked Jack.

'Yeah,' I said, pleased at the thought. 'It's like a riddle from me to you.'

He thought for a moment, as I fiddled with the page of my exercise book. Just then, the 10.15 p.m. to New York appeared in the corner of Jack's skylight and we both looked up, amazed that it was still there, even after everything else had changed.

'I think that Lady Abigail and Margot reunite, but she stays working at the hospital. That's what I *want* to happen,' he clarified.

'Why?'

'Because I think it's important to do what you believe in. Even if it's not what other people want you to do. You need some guts, but I reckon Margot has plenty of guts.'

'Ha! Maybe it's because she's based on you.'

'Is she? I didn't know,' he said, pulling a face.

'Of course you did,' I said. 'You knew from the moment that I started reading, didn't you?'

'Well, maybe we share some similarities,' he said grinning. 'I hope that we both end up doing something awesome. So…? Will you tell me what happens?'

I kept glancing at him, smiling, as I read:

Lady Abigail spotted Margot as soon as she walked through the door. She was dressed in a greying apron which made her look much older than she was, and she was leaning over a cot, swaddling the baby tightly against the cold. Then she gazed down at its little face with a look of happiness and love. Lady Abigail realised with a start that she hadn't seen that expression on her daughter's face in years.

Margot jumped when she saw her mother. 'What are you doing here?' she asked, alarmed and slightly frightened.

'Looking for you,' Lady Abigail whispered. 'Why didn't you tell me where you were going?'

Margot took a long time to answer.

'I thought that you wouldn't understand,' she said finally, looking down at the floor. 'And I was worried that you might try to stop me coming. I love it, you see... I know that you think it's a dirty and thankless job, but I love it.'

'I wouldn't have prevented you...' Lady Abigail started, and then she stopped herself, knowing that it wasn't true. She pulled her daughter close. 'I'm sorry,' she said into her hair. 'I've missed you. I was so worried. I want more than anything for you to come back.'

'I'd love to come home, but I also want to stay working here.' Margot's voice was shaking. If she didn't say it now, she never would.

Lady Abigail looked at her daughter hopefully.

'It's possible to do both though, isn't it?'

When Margot's smile appeared, it radiated warmth and happiness.

'It is, absolutely.'

'Let's all have dinner together tonight, and tomorrow I'll walk you to work on the way to do my errands. What do you say?' asked Lady Abigail nervously.

'I say "yes".'

And Lady Abigail kept her promise. The following morning, her own purple bonnet could be seen bobbing next to Margot's red beret, as they made their way through the bustling London streets towards the Evelina Children's Hospital.

I finished reading and looked at Jack.

He was smiling. 'Another riddle solved,' he said. 'Good work, Sergeant Flick, good work.'

Acknowledgements

Thank you to my fantastic publishers and editors Fiona Kennedy and Lauren Atherton at Zephyr, who responded to my story with their characteristic encouragement and support; to Jessie, Clare, Chrissy and the rest of the wonderful Head of Zeus family who helped me to form the bones of this story before I had even begun writing it.

Thank you to my hugely knowledgeable and ever-supportive agent Kate Hordern for her unfailing optimism, wise words, and good advice.

Thank you to Cat and Joe who described to me exactly how overwhelming and frightening experiencing an earthquake is, and to Peru Travel for their invaluable insight into the country's geography – any location discrepancies are entirely my own.

Thank you to my friends and family, and all my young readers who make writing stories the best thing in the world, particularly to Scarlett, Max, Erin, Isla and Imogen who gave me some super feedback.

Ewa Jozefkowicz
London, 2020

Coming in Spring 2021

The Cooking Club Detectives
by Ewa Jozefkowicz

Erin's mum, Lara, gets a job as a cookery
teacher at their local community centre.
Erin loves the cooking club, where she makes
new friends and tries out lots of tasty recipes with
them. But suddenly the community centre is under
threat. Who could be plotting against them and
why? Erin, her new puppy Sausages,
and her friends turn detective to solve
the mystery and find out
what's going on.

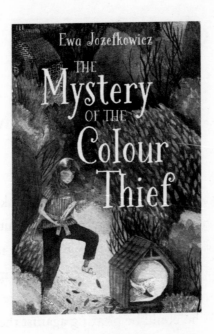

Out now in paperback

First the accident, then the nightmares and the thief who steals the colour from Izzy's world. Will her neighbour and a nest of cygnets help solve the mystery of the colour thief? A heartwarming story about families, friendships, school, nature, hope and self-confidence.

'A really impressive nuanced debut looking at how to cope with and survive life.'
The Bookseller

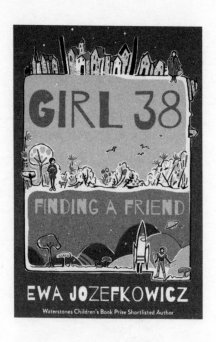

Out now in paperback

Past and present are woven into the second
middle grade novel by Ewa Jozefkowicz, set in
contemporary times and WWII Poland. Based on
a real life story, about friendship and endurance
in the darkest situation.

'*Girl 38* has strong themes of bullying, friendship
and difference, but the author's light touch balances
the deeper issues with a lot of heart.'
BookTrust